MW01125792

SWEET BITTER FREEDOM

the enthralling sequel
to The Throwback

David Canford

Mad-books.com

DAVID CANFORD

COPYRIGHT © 2018 DAVID CANFORD

1.21

All rights reserved. No part of this publication may be reproduced, distributed, or transmitted in any form or by any means, or stored in a database or retrieval system, without the prior written permission of the author.

This novel is a work of fiction and a product of the author's imagination. Any resemblance to anyone living or dead (save for named historical figures) or any entity or legal person is purely coincidental and unintended.

Cover Design By: Mary Ann Dujardin

Sign up to receive David Canford's email newsletter at DavidCanford.com for information on new book releases, promotions and claim your free ebook.

CHAPTER 1

Mosa had never expected to be staring down the barrel of a gun again now that the Civil War had ended, and certainly not one which was held by a Union soldier.

His navy blue jacket and light blue pants were holed and smeared with dirt. The man was agitated and unpredictable, the barrel moving slightly from side to side. Yet it hadn't begun like this.

"Hey, Mosa. Get yourself over here."

The joy in Joshua's voice was evident. Mosa had got up from her knees in the vegetable patch she had been tending, wiping her callused hands on her old dress to remove as much of the soil from them as she could.

She no longer had the smooth hands of the New York teacher who she had once been. They were all in this together, toiling each and every day to ensure that everyone who remained on the plantation got fed. The war may have been won but the peace was proving every bit as much of a struggle. Reaching Joshua's side, she noticed his mother,

Maisie, hovering a few inches above the ground as the man who had lifted her up embraced her.

"It's my brother, Jacob. He's alive." Joshua's grin was wide and full.

Jacob had altered from when Mosa had last seen him over five years ago. No longer a lanky teenager, his shoulders were broad, and he was now taller than his brother, although other than in height they were very similar.

After Jacob had returned their mother to earth, the two brothers hugged.

"Man, it's so good to see you, Jacob."

"You too. Who's this with you?"

"You remember Mosa, don't you?"

"The house girl who got sold away?"

"Hello, Jacob."

"Mosa, yes I remember you. Hope you don't mind me asking, but was it the Elwoods that did that to you?"

Mosa touched her cheek, feeling once again the damaged skin displaying the indelible "R" for runaway which had been burned onto her flesh as if she were a farm animal.

"No, it happened down in Georgia, but Thomas got me out of there."

Mosa had learned to live with her disfigurement. She had decided some while ago that she'd cried too many tears over things she couldn't ever change. People she had loved and lost, awful experiences she had endured. It was time to focus on the future, not the past. That could never be changed. But the future, that held possibilities now that they had all been freed at last.

"Do you have any news of your brother, Silas?" asked Maisie, her eyes showing both hope and fear, not knowing what his answer would be.

"No, Mama. I'm sorry, I don't. He got sent to Virginia and me to Tennessee. We can't write, you know that, so there was no way of keeping in touch."

"Well, the good Lord saw fit to bring you home. That means he's been listening to my prayers. I'll keep on praying Silas is safe and makes it back too. Come with me and let's get some food in you. You look thin."

"In a minute. What happened to the Elwoods. Did they flee? I can see the house got burned down."

Although it was already three months since that had happened, the ground where their mansion had once stood remained scorched and lifeless, the result of the battle here between the opposing armies.

"No, old man Elwood died, and then Thomas got shot by that son of a bitch overseer, O'Connell," answered Joshua.

"Well, at least none of us has to fight them to take what is rightfully ours."

"What do you mean?"

"What I mean, brother, is this land is now ours. It belongs to us and every man who was once a slave here. It's our recompense for all they did to us and our forebears. We've earned it with our blood, sweat, and tears, forced to work for them every day since we could walk without so much as a cent in return."

"But you can't just take someone else's land."

"Yes, we damn well can. If not, what did so many die fighting for?"

"To free us."

"And what good will that have been if the land is left with them that oppressed us? Having to work for them for next to nothing. How will that make us free?"

"Your brother's got a point there," said one of the men from amongst the thirty or so former slaves who still lived there and had gathered to watch the family reunion.

"This land belongs to Mosa," said Joshua. "Thomas left it all to her. She risked her life during the war to get back here from up North, and has taught us all to read and write so we'd have an advantage when freedom came. Once this place is up and running again, she's promised half of the profit to the rest of us."

"Is that so. Why does she get to keep a whole half for herself? Anyway, why should just one person have all this land?"

"Yeah," agreed some of the bystanders.

"Joshua done married her to make sure he's OK," added one of them.

"Well, congratulations to you brother, and you too, Mosa, but we all deserve a piece of this land."

"Look, Jacob, I'm real glad that you survived and

we'd be happy for you to join us and live here. Live here on the same terms as everyone else. But I won't have you come here causing trouble. If you don't like my offer, you can leave," said Joshua.

"I ain't leaving. I didn't go to hell and back fighting the Confederates to just walk away. I've come to claim what's mine and that's that."

"Don't make me fight you, Jacob. I'd still beat you, just like when we were kids."

Jacob said nothing in reply but took the rifle which he carried off his shoulder. "I don't want to hurt you, brother, but we're all gonna share in the fruits of victory, not just a privileged few. You either accept that, or you need to leave and go be somebody's nigger someplace else."

He now had the rifle pointing at Joshua and Mosa, who was standing by his side. Only the annoying buzzing of the mosquitoes disturbed the still, humid air as everyone watched with bated breath to see what would happen next.

"What's it gonna be, brother?"

"No, Jacob. Stop this right now," said Maisie.

"Stay out of this Mama. It's between Joshua and me."

Mosa intervened.

"Let him have his way. This place ain't worth dying for."

"Well said, sister-in-law. Come on, Joshua. We'll divide it up into equal shares for everyone. Surely you gotta agree that's fair."

"It's OK, Joshua, really it is," said Mosa softly as she

took his arm, hoping that the way he was standing with his jaw aggressively thrust out and his hands on his hips didn't signal an intent to fight and risk being shot.

"Hmm."

Joshua stomped off toward their cabin like an old lion whose place in the pride had been usurped by a younger, stronger male. As the rest stood around Jacob, their new hero, chatting excitedly, Mosa departed to be with her husband.

CHAPTER 2

Their home was basic, nothing like the grandeur of the house which Mosa had inherited when her brother, Thomas, had died. Yet Mosa didn't mind. This place was truly hers, hers and Joshua's. She'd never really felt comfortable in the big house. It had been a constant reminder of those who had lived there and enslaved them. They may have been dead but it was as though their malign spirits had never left and were woven into the very fabric of that building.

Inside the couple's dwelling there was just their bed, a table, a couple of upright chairs, and a cupboard, all made from the same rough wood as the cabin itself. However, it was enough. After all, they had no stuff to speak of. Nothing had been salvaged from the fire. Not even the books which Mosa had valued more than all the fine furniture. The conflagration had been too great to rescue anything.

In a way it had been fitting, almost like a biblical event. An end to the old order, collapsing violently just as the Confederacy had. As if God had intervened, wanting to erase the evil which had existed before.

But freedom was proving to be as bitter as it was sweet. The barn holding all the cotton, which Mosa had planned to sell when the war ended to raise money to keep the plantation going, had also been set alight. Those here lived hand to mouth, depending on a few hogs and chickens and the vegetables which they grew to feed themselves. It was subsistence living.

The South lay in ruins. Its railroads were no more, nearly half its livestock was gone. Disease and starvation stalked the land, disproportionately affecting African Americans. As always, it was the poorest who suffered the most. They remained unprotected, vulnerable to murder and rape just as before, probably even more so. Many whites hated them with a vengeance, blamed them for their severely reduced circumstances, and resented what they saw as their lack of gratitude for having given them a place to live and food to eat.

Mosa had been shocked to see the scale of devastation when she and Joshua had taken the horse and cart into Columbia, the State capital, last month. Controversy still raged whether the fire which had almost leveled it, had been started by the Confederates or General Sherman's men. Whatever the truth, his men had certainly finished the job, destroying all the public buildings which remained. The partially completed new State House was severely damaged, and the old one from where secession had first begun was no more.

While the Northerners could congratulate themselves on ending slavery, they hadn't followed through with the support needed to give those who were its victims the tools needed to make a success of their freedom. Nor would they welcome the black population of the South moving North in search of opportunity and a better life. Mosa already knew from first hand experience that up there they were also seen as a threat, people who would come take the jobs of white folk for less pay. A narrative which was ruthlessly promoted by politicians seeking to rouse the masses and garner their votes.

Here on Old Oaks plantation in South Carolina, Mosa and the rest were more fortunate than many. They could get by. Just.

Joshua was slumped in a chair when she pushed open the door. His greeting was a frown.

"Why did you just let him take it off you like that?"

"Like what? Did you want me to resist and see you get shot. You're worth more to me than any piece of land. Anyway, perhaps he's right. If colored folk are ever going to get on in this world, they need land they can work for their own benefit."

"But you've been more than fair. They've taken advantage of your good nature."

"Maybe. But let's be happy for what we've got. We've a roof over our head and food to eat, and we have each other. And best of all, we're finally free. For the very first time, we have control of our future."

Joshua half laughed, half grunted before getting up to give her a cuddle.

"You sure are a special lady."

"And you're a special man, Joshua. Now, if you'll let me go, I'll fix us something to eat."

The following morning, they joined Jacob and the others outside. Joshua was pleased to see his brother had swapped his uniform for ordinary clothes. Walking around in these parts in such shades of blue was inviting trouble.

"I'm told there are eight families here, so by my reckoning we should divide the land into eight equal parts."

"And how do you propose to do that? Did they teach you math in the Union army?" asked Joshua. Jacob ignored the sarcasm.

"It's not difficult. We just measure it out in paces, and our very own teacher, your beautiful wife that is, can calculate how much we each get. What do you say?"

The men in the crowd other than Joshua voiced their agreement.

"And what about the hogs and chickens. How will you divide them? Chop them into eight separate pieces?" Joshua challenged him.

"Can I suggest we treat them as a combined re-source. The eggs can be shared out and when we agree to kill a pig, the meat can be handed out equally."

"Sounds like an excellent idea to me, Mosa," said Jacob.

By the end of the day, they had divided the plantation. Not that they had anything to farm it with. No one had any money to buy any cottonseed or other supplies. They were masters of nothing.

As the sun sunk in the west, a woman came walking up the path from that direction. A small child held one of her hands and her other hand carried a bag.

Mosa was used to passers-by seeking food. The men would normally see them off with their rifles at the ready just in case. There were many desperate souls out there, prepared to kill if necessary to find something to eat. It pained her that they couldn't help. The subdued look of exhaustion on children's faces and despair in the eyes of their parents were heartbreaking. Yet if they fed all those who came begging, they would go hungry themselves.

A woman and a child posed no threat so Mosa didn't call for the men and went to meet the lady herself. Her features had been hidden by the long shadows of evening and the sun behind her. As Mosa got closer, she could see that the woman was white and red-headed. Her hair was long and untidy, her pale cheeks a mass of freckles. The boy with her also had his mother's hair color and complexion. By the way they hobbled as if their feet must be sore and blistered, it appeared they must have been wandering around for some time.

DAVID CANFORD

"I'm sorry but we can't take you in or feed you. We're hungry ourselves. You'll have to leave. Go back the way you came."

The woman didn't retreat.

"I'm Lowenna and this is my son, Abraham."

The blank expression on Mosa's face indicated that their names meant nothing to her.

"Lowenna Jenkins. Lloyd's wife. The owner of the plantation wrote to me."

Mosa remembered. She had fulfilled Lloyd's dying wish that she write to his wife. She still recalled the words.

Dear Mrs. Jenkins

It is with the greatest of regret that I must inform you of the passing of your brave husband, Lloyd. He and his soldiers were involved in a fight with Confederates here at the plantation.

I appreciate that this will come as a terrible shock and bring you great pain. I send you my heartfelt condolences for your loss.

I hope it will bring you some solace to know that your husband was a hero. You can rightly be proud of him. He fought bravely for a noble cause.

His dying wish was that I should write to you, to tell you just how much he loved you and your son.

Should you ever be in need, you and your son will always be welcome here at my plantation. We don't have a great deal, but I will gladly share with you what we do have for we shall forever be in your husband's debt.

"Please could you take me to the owner, Miss Mosa Elwood."

"I am she."

Lowenna moved her head back in surprise.

"Oh, I hadn't been expecting a...er..."

She struggled to come up with the appropriate word.

"It's all right, I understand. I'm probably the only non-white person in the entire county, if not the State, that owned a plantation."

"Well, I hope you don't mind me turning up. I'm guessing you didn't receive my letter to say I was coming to take you up on your kind invitation."

"No, the mail is pretty unreliable. But no matter, I am delighted to make your acquaintance and you are both most welcome."

"Thank you. I shall be glad to have a bed to sleep in and a bath. It's been a long and arduous journey. You must have a very large plantation. I can't even see the house."

CHAPTER 3

"What do mean you asked her here?" demanded Joshua.

He and Mosa were inside the cabin, arguing in quiet voices, conscious that Lowenna was only a few feet away on the other side of the wall.

"It was the least I could do. Her husband gave his life for us to be free. She needs our help. Seems their marriage was never properly registered. The government refused her a widow's pension and she didn't know what to do so she spent what money she had left to come down here. Imagine her disappointment. She thought she was coming to stay in a mansion. When I wrote to her, I never went into detail about all that had happened."

"And I don't suppose you mentioned that Lloyd had promised to marry you either."

"No, of course not. Why would I? I was pleased he had married as I'd fallen in love with you and I didn't need to feel guilty that I'd be letting him down. Anyway, we can't throw her and her kid out. We've spare huts."

"We have but Jacob and the rest sure aren't gonna

agree to sharing. Especially with white folk."

"Maybe not but I'll have a word with them, and remind them about what Lloyd did. If we all cling tightly to what little we have and don't share, things will stay that way and we'll be the poorer for it. The past was all about that. White folk wanted to keep it all for themselves, and remember what that was like. Just because those who once owned us showed no humanity, we don't have to be like them."

"OK, do as you wish. We've already lost the plantation. Her being here won't change that."

Outside, Lowenna stood smiling a little anxiously at the sea of curious faces staring at her and her son.

"Hey, everyone," began Mosa as she emerged. "This here is Lowenna Jenkins, wife of Captain Lloyd Jenkins and their son, Abraham. I'm sure you haven't forgotten how Lloyd led his troops in the battle when we'd been kidnapped by O'Connell and his rabble. How he gave his own life to save us from those bad men. I wrote to Lowenna to give her the sad news, and let her know she and her boy would always be welcome if ever they were in need."

"But we don't have enough for ourselves. We've turned more deserving away, plenty of folk like us."

"Come on, Jobe. Let's leave color out of this. That's what the slave owners did. Condemned us because of our color. We're better than that."

Maisie stepped forward.

"I agree with Mosa. If Lloyd and his men hadn't come, we'd all have been burned alive in that barn. Those Confederate soldiers were never gonna let us out. That O' Connell was pure evil. I got scars on my back to prove it as have most of you."

"Yeah, he sure was," agreed several of the other women.

The men looked at Jacob, waiting to see his reaction. He was their leader now.

"Seems to me we should let her stay. We owe her husband that. I met many good white guys in the Union army. Many bad ones too. But sounds like Captain Jenkins was in the good camp. Though I say she's Mosa's responsibility to feed, and she and Joshua shouldn't get any extra for that."

"No, son. If you're gonna be that mean, she and her baby can have my share and I'll go without. I didn't raise you and your brothers to behave like this. And if it weren't for Mosa agreeing to come back, the plantation would've been sold off to only the Lord knows who. There's no doubt in my mind that we wouldn't have been treated anywhere near as good. So you and the others need to make your decision, but I won't be changing my mind."

Though diminutive in stature, a hard life had molded Maisie into a formidable character, but formidable in the best possible way. She was kind and generous to a fault. For the first time since his arrival, Jacob looked uncertain of himself.

"OK, you win. I can't watch my own mother starve and I know you mean what you say. You always have been stubborn as a mule."

"Stubborn yes, but I ain't no mule," said Mosa standing on her toes and clipping his ear. "And maybe that'll remind you not to disrespect your Mama."

"Yes ma'am."

"Good. Mosa, I'll go sweep out one of the empty cabins if you tell me which one."

"Thank you, Maisie. You're the best. Maybe that one over there. It's in a better state of repair. I'll get Lowenna and Abraham some food. Come with me, you must both be hungry after your journey."

In the early hours, Mosa was awoken by singing. The voice was a baritone, one that could have been enjoyable if the singer hadn't been drunk and it hadn't also been the middle of the night. Joshua got up and went outside.

"Keep the noise down, will you. The rest of us are trying to get a good night's sleep before another day's hard work. Looking at the state of you, you won't be any help. If you want to be a landowner, you need to start behaving like one."

"Lighten up brother. You always were a misery. I've just been drinking with friends who I met on the neighboring plantation. Celebrating our freedom. At least they treated me with respect. They appreciate my service. If it weren't for the likes of me, you'd all still be slaves, picking cotton and bowing your heads. Yes Mas'r, no Mas'r."

"I'd keep your mouth shut about being in the Union army if I were you. People talk. White folk damn sure won't appreciate your service. There's only one thing they hate more than a Yankee, a former slave who fought for the North."

Though most days she worked from dawn to dusk, Mosa would occasionally treat herself to a break and wander off. She no longer told Joshua, who had asked her not to go alone.

He was right that it carried a risk, especially for a young woman like her. Even with emancipation, the chances of any white man being charged for attacking a black person were negligible. And in the unlikely event a prosecution was ever brought, the all white male jury was never going to convict one of their own. However, Mosa had lived in fear before, had felt it drain her of confidence and make her feel without hope. She didn't ever want to live her life that way again.

On this occasion, she had asked Lowenna if she would like to walk with her. They meandered along the river bank, enjoying the soft soporific sound of the water as it passed by. It seemed as far from trouble as you could get. A sanctuary of liquid balm, and a world away from reality.

Yet to Mosa it revived memories that belied its apparently benign nature. It was the very same river Mosa was supposed to have been thrown into as a baby, the river from which she had rescued Thomas from drowning, and the river she had had to take her chances on and cross when she had tried to escape. So much of what had happened in her life had been linked to this spot.

Although there was two of them, the pounding of cantering hooves coming from behind caused them both to halt and sent an involuntary shudder down Mosa's back as they turned around to see who it was.

CHAPTER 4

The rider had almost reached them. He yanked on the reins of his horse, coming to an abrupt halt. Mosa had difficulty making out the face under the broad-brimmed hat the man wore until he tipped it back.

"Good day to you, Mosa."

"Mr. Brown."

It was Gregory Brown, the owner of the adjacent plantation, and her first owner. His thin lips and narrow eyes hinted at the mean spirit residing within him.

"And who, may I ask, is this beautiful lady?"

His voice left the slimy trail of a slug hanging in the air.

"Lowenna Jenkins, the widow of Captain Jenkins who so valiantly saved us all from being burned alive by the Confederate army."

"Lowenna. What a pretty name. Well, now you're in the South, my dear, you'll be able to find yourself a fine Southern husband. You don't want to be spending time with niggers though. Decent folk will take a dim view of that and it will damage your prospects."

Lowenna's cheeks reddened.

"I find your assumption impertinent, sir. I didn't come here to find a husband, and I am most grateful to Mosa for her kind hospitality. If folk think like you say they do, I can't see how they can claim to be decent. I'd better be getting back, Mosa, to check on Abe."

"I'll come with."

"There was something I wanted to talk to you about," interrupted Brown.

"You go ahead," said Mosa to Lowenna. "I'll be back soon."

"My, she's a feisty one." Brown watched her go, a lascivious look on his face. "What you get up to never ceases to amaze me."

"What is it you wanted to talk to me about?"

"I hear tell you've let the niggers run riot on your place, seize your land off you."

"That's not how I'd put it."

"Your kind just don't understand the value of property, do you. My slaves, well they used to be mine until the world lost its mind, wanted to take my land off of me too. I dealt with that. I only had to shoot a couple to make them back off.

"My offer to buy your place still stands, though of course land values have dropped even further since I made it so I can't be quite as generous as before. Still, you'd walk away with enough money to live in comfort for the rest of your days. What do you say?"

DAVID CANFORD

"Like I said already, it's not for sale."
"As you wish, but think on it carefully. By the time you're wanting to sell, it'll be all but worthless. Meanwhile, I have some good news for you. President Johnson - I do take it that you know he's the new President after Lincoln got what he had coming to him."
"I had heard. And to my mind it is an absolute tragedy that President Lincoln was assassinated after freeing so many people. However, I take comfort from knowing that he will be remembered and revered for so long as the United States shall exist, unlike lesser men who will soon be forgotten."
Inwardly, Mosa despaired. Brown wasn't an outlier. He represented majority white opinion across the South. The physical battles may have ended. The battle to win over people's minds had yet to be fought, and seemed an impossible one to win.
"Well, you'd better start respecting President Johnson too. He started life as a Southerner and a Democrat so he understands what's needed now. He doesn't have his heart set on punishing the South because he knows that will lead to further conflict. The man has now decreed that all land in the South which was confiscated is to be returned to its rightful owners. So that'll help you out. The law's back on your side. If you need help to deal with the uppity niggers you got on your plantation, I'll be happy to come on over with some of my men to assist. Just say the word.

"And to show that I've got your best interests at heart, I've a piece of advice you'd do well to heed. There's a new system of farming taking root that'll protect you and your land. It's called sharecropping. I'm going to try it out myself. You, as landowner, let your former slaves use your land in return for giving you a good share of what they produce. There are businesses springing up all over who'll advance supplies on credit to niggers. And at the end of the day, if it don't work out or you want to grow cotton again, you can kick them off your land."

"It sounds like exploitation to me, only one step up from slavery."

"You can be an idealist if you want, but it won't put food on your table or enable you to keep your land in the long term. You're just as pigheaded as you always were my girl."

Mosa bit her tongue. There was nothing to be gained by responding. He was a man who didn't listen. Only making a success of the plantation would show men like him what she and those like her were capable of if they were given the opportunity.

"I must be getting back. Goodbye."

Mosa marched off swiftly, her afternoon spoiled.

"I'm sorry about Gregory Brown," she said when she caught up with Lowenna back on the plantation. "He has a big mouth and an even bigger ego."

"Don't worry. I've met plenty of men like him before. I often think the good ones like Lloyd and

Joshua are in the minority."

"I'm afraid he's right about what white folk will think. Maybe for your sake you should consider leaving and finding a life amongst them."

"Well, I don't want to be a burden-"

"Oh, no, that's not what I meant. I love having you here so long as you don't mind being ostracized by your own kind."

Mosa worried about Lowenna. She often appeared sad, lost in introspection. Of course, she must still miss her husband. Mosa felt guilty that she hadn't been more explicit about the circumstances here. Having spent most of her life living like she did now, she didn't really think about it that much. She should have appreciated that to Lowenna how they lived would have come as a shock. She probably would never had made the trip down here if Mosa had been more open with her about what she would find.

When Mosa had written that letter, her mind had been on other things. The house had just been destroyed and all their stores of cotton too. With the benefit of hindsight, her invitation to Lowenna had probably been misguided.

Later that day, Mosa came across Lowenna sitting in the shade of a tree, her knees pulled up and her head resting on them like a lost child.

"Are you all right, Lowenna?"

She looked up, her expression one of embarrassment at having been found. Her eyes were red from recent crying.

"Yes. It's nothing."

"Well, folk don't normally get upset about nothing so it must be something. You can tell me, I'm your friend. You know what they say, a problem shared is a problem halved."

"I feel me and Abe are just a nuisance. We shouldn't have come. We'd get out of your way if we could, but I spent everything I had left to pay for the journey."

"You mustn't think like that. Like I said, you're always welcome here. We owe it to Lloyd. You know, you sure have a pretty way of talking. I've been meaning to ask which part of the country you were born in."

"I wasn't. I'm from Cornwall in the southwest corner of England."

"That sounds like a nice place. What brought you to America?"

"Things were tough there too. My family were poor and we often went hungry. I stole a loaf of bread as it lay cooling on the window ledge of someone's kitchen window sill. They sentenced me to transportation to Australia. I escaped from jail before the boat left and stowed away on one coming across the Atlantic, and ended up in Washington shortly before the war started. I was only sixteen at the time."

"Do you miss home?"

"Sometimes, though I've no kith and kin to go back to. My parents are dead now, and my brothers died of disease. I do miss the climate. Summers were way more pleasant back home. It never gets anywhere near as hot as it does here. Washington was like this, airless and sticky."

"I'm used to it, I guess. It's all I've ever known apart from some time I spent in New York. That was humid too but extremely cold come winter."

"New York. That's where Lloyd came from."

"Really. I have things I must do. Will you be OK?"

"Yeah, of course."

Mosa scolded herself for not telling Lowenna that she'd known Lloyd in New York, nor that she was to be his wife. But then why? What good would that do, other than make Lowenna feel awkward and even more unhappy to be here. Some things were best left unsaid.

One hundred miles away on the coast, a couple strolled arm in arm along the waterfront relishing the cooling breeze coming off the water, a welcome relief from the ferocious heat. He had been an attorney's clerk, she once a society lady. Like the rubble which lay in piles around the city of Charleston from over five hundred days of bombardment, their lives until recently had also seemed to be in ruins.

She had fallen on hard times when her home had received a direct hit from a shell fired from a Union vessel shortly before the fall of the city. Her parents had been killed. Out at the time, she had survived. As for him, he had been fired from the offices of Matthias Coburg on suspicion of attempting to steal clients' money, a suspicion which he knew to be true.

But fate had been kind. When he had left Columbia and moved to Charleston, she and he had met and become lovers. And more than that, they had discovered a happy coincidence from their past lives. One which could see their fortunes restored.

CHAPTER 5

Gregory Brown had been right. President Johnson went easy on the South. The plantation elite remained in control. His only demand was that they accept the Thirteenth Amendment abolishing slavery, promising to then leave them alone.

In elections, largely the same people who had ruled during the Confederacy were elected. Those freed from slavery had no right to vote. Once South Carolina had ratified the Thirteenth in November 1865 it, like the other rebel States, passed the Black Codes to severely control and restrict the rights of the freed slaves. One such tactic were the vagrancy laws, allowing unemployed black men to be jailed and hired out to work for free. The alternative, having to sign labor contracts heavily biased in favor of the employer, wasn't a whole lot better.

The once wealthy South had been built on the back of slavery. Their former owners conceived this new system of oppression, worried that without coercion freedmen might not be willing to work for them any longer.

The assumption that the Civil War brought freedom to all was in reality nothing more than a cruel deception. Southern whites having lost the war were determined to win the peace whatever it might require and however long it may take.

On the Old Oaks Plantation, there existed the illusion of freedom. They were self-contained, living in a bubble. They rarely had to interact with the ruling class.

Mosa relayed to Joshua what Gregory Brown had told her.

"Like you, I wouldn't want to introduce sharecropping, but none of us are going to get anywhere with what we've got going on right now. We need a loan to achieve anything, and no bank is gonna lend us eight loans for eight small pieces of land. But if the land was under your control again maybe they would. I'll have a word with Mama. Perhaps she can talk some sense into Jacob."

That evening, Mosa, Joshua, and Jacob sat out under the stars as the hooting of owls and croaking of frogs made the night a little magical. The others sat around in their own small groups, some near the fire which had been lit.

"So tell me, Mosa, how come Thomas left it all to you? Did you have some hold over him?" asked Jacob.

"No. Guess he just had no one else left that he wanted to leave it to."

Only Maisie and Joshua knew her true parentage. She hadn't thought it a good idea to share the family secret with everyone. Acceptance hadn't come easily for Mosa, and she was concerned the truth would adversely change people's perception of her.

"Maybe it's because you're an Elwood." Mosa blushed, though in the semi-darkness of the fire-light Jacob didn't notice. "Like we're all goddamn Elwoods. When I got over the battle lines and signed up, they wanted to know my last name. I said Elwood. What else were we supposed to be? Whatever family each of us were once part of, we'll never know. I've thought about changing it for something more noble. Lincoln perhaps. What's your view, Joshua?"

"I think we have bigger worries than a name right now."

"You would. Have you ever thought about going to Africa? In the army they told us about Liberia, a country established by abolitionists for our folk. They said we should consider it, that things could be a whole lot better there for us. No white folk seeking to exploit us and keep us down."

"That's what they tell you, but who knows what it's like until you get there. It ain't like going to an-other State. Africa's far away and a big place. None of us know which part our ancestors were stolen from and where home really was. Anyhow, Mama wouldn't want to go, and I couldn't leave her here all alone."

"Well, it's what I intend to do someday. It's the one place we might finally find peace and freedom."

Flickering lights amongst the trees, like the bio-luminescence of fireflies, caught their attention. Out of the indigo night, several horses appeared. Some of their riders carried torches. All bore rifles. They wore pillowcases over their faces to hide their identities.

Mosa's heart began racing. They'd all heard reports of former Confederate soldiers terrorizing the black population, the forerunners of the KKK, Ku Klux Klan.

Those on the plantation were as defenseless as cubs out in the open. The few rifles which they had between them weren't within reach, and in any event a shootout would bring only temporary relief. The intruders would be back with a bigger force the next time.

There was an ominous silence as the man who appeared to be in charge scanned those there. Although his face was hidden, the menace of it was apparent as his pupils stared through the two eye-holes.

"What are you doing here?"

The man's gaze had settled on Lowenna as her son enveloped himself as much as he possibly could in the folds of her dress, terrified by these demons on horseback.

"Me?...oh, I was on my way to Columbia when my horse became lame," she lied. "These kind people have fed us and cared for us. Please don't harm them. They are good, law-abiding citizens."

"Citizens? Niggers ain't citizens and never will be.

And the company of niggers is no place for a white woman. You can accompany us when we're done here and we'll get you to Columbia. Climb on the back of that horse there."

Lowenna got up from the ground to comply. It had been easy to challenge Gregory Brown's bigotry. Defying a gang of armed men was a different matter. The rider on the horse helped her and her son up. The leader then turned his attention to the others.

"Which one of you here served in the Union army?" No one replied. "You'd better answer my question, or we'll take every one of your men."

"I did."

Mosa stifled a cry. Joshua had stood up.

"No, brother, you can't do this for me," said Jacob as he leaped to his feet. "It was me. Jacob Elwood. I was proud to serve."

"Tie him," commanded the man.

Two of the renegades jumped down and tied his hands together and then the rope to the reins of one of the horses.

"Please, sir, please. Don't do this, don't hurt my baby. The war's over now."

Maisie had approached the man.

"Get out of my way woman!"

There was a swish of air as he drew back his switch and brought it down across her face. The force of it caused her to stagger backward and fall over. Mosa hurried across and held Maisie in her arms as the gang turned and sped away.

Jacob ran to keep up with the horses but they were too fast for him. Before they'd disappeared into the night, he'd been pulled over and was being dragged along the ground like a plaything. After they were out of sight, the light from the burning torches remained visible for some while until that too disappeared as if it had all only been a bad dream that those on the plantation would soon wake up from.

"I'm going to find him," said Jacob.

"No, it's too late. I can't risk losing another son. Wait till morning. I'm going inside to pray, pray that the good Lord will let him live."

As the first streaks of dawn appeared in the East, Joshua set out on Shadow, the faithful horse that had belonged to Thomas. Two other men accompanied him. Once off the plantation they advanced cautiously, ready to vanish into the forest if they saw any insurgents.

A mile or two down the rutted dirt road as the rising sun turned from orange to a blinding ball of light, they saw him silhouetted by the sun's rays like a saint in a religious painting. But it was no picture of glory. His body hung lifeless, covered in cuts and dirt. His head was down, his chin on his chest.

The men dismounted. His whole body shaking, Joshua climbed up onto the shoulders of one of the men who had crouched down for him to do so. The man stood up, holding Joshua by the ankles. As he cut the rope, the other man with them caught the body as it fell, laying it gently down on the earth. The man holding Joshua crouched once more so Joshua could jump off his shoulders.

Jacob's eyes were still open. After wiping his arm across his face to remove his tears, Joshua closed his brother's eyelids.

Maisie let out a haunting wail of desolation as she saw them return. Jacob was lying across Joshua. He held him in his arms as he let his horse walk slowly toward their mother. After the others had taken him off Joshua and put Jacob down on the ground, she threw herself on him, her whole body convulsing as she sobbed and repeatedly called his name.

CHAPTER 6

Jacob was buried next to his father. The shock of her son's murder was to turn Maisie's hair gray almost overnight.

As they lay in bed, Mosa ran her fingers gently over the scars on Joshua's back as she held him in his grief. She too had a back which told her story. Both of them had once tried to escape from here and had paid the price of failure.

Now they were free to leave but after a war costing a million lives their world remained a hostile place. Mosa fretted what their future would be now that there would be added responsibility. She had planned on sharing her news with Joshua the night they came for Jacob. However, it was no longer the right time. Maybe she would tell him in a few days.

She waited for Lowenna to return but she didn't. Mosa hoped that was for a good reason, that she had found a place to stay and was safe.

It was as Joshua and she stood by Jacob's grave having laid some fresh flowers that they heard a sound which they had come to fear more than any other.

The approach of a horse, perhaps more than one. They turned, their eyes filled with dread as to who it might be.

On this occasion it was just one man in a black suit, a brown bag strung over his shoulder.

"I've come to see a Miss Elwood, Miss Mosa Elwood."

Mosa stepped forward.

"You are she?"

"I am. What is it that you want?"

Reaching into his bag, he pulled out an envelope.

"This is for you."

Instinctively, she reached out and took it.

"You have been served. Good day to you."

"What now?" asked Joshua.

"I've no idea. I'm going inside to open it."

She read the document with increasing concern. It was from the courts of Richland County, in the matter of Thomas Edward Elwood deceased. A Mrs. Emma Elizabeth Elwood was petitioning to have the last will and testament of Thomas set aside on grounds of him being of unsound mind for bequeathing his estate to one Mosa Elwood, a former slave. Further, the court was being asked to rule that his earlier will should therefore take effect leaving his estate to his father and should his father predecease him as he had, then to his father's wife and his stepmother, the said Mrs. Emma Elwood.

Mosa felt lightheaded. She read it again, not sure if she might have misunderstood. Joshua came in.

"Whatever is the matter? You look like you've seen a ghost."

"Read this."

Joshua said the words out loud as he read.

"But they can't do this. He left the plantation to you. You were his sister. There's nothing insane about leaving property to your sister."

"No, there isn't. But we have no proof. I don't have any birth certificate. What judge is gonna believe what I say?"

"When's the hearing?"

"There's another letter here. It says the end of next month in Columbia."

"Didn't you once say it was the grandmother who confirmed you were the Elwood's child, that there was African blood in the family?"

"Yes, Clarissa. She lived in Charleston but she may well be dead by now. Even if she ain't, I don't place much hope on her helping. She gave that confirmation to save Thomas from hanging when he sprung me off the plantation in Georgia I'd been sold to, in the knowledge that a statement given to a judge there wasn't going to be public knowledge in this State. She wanted my existence to be kept a secret, made Thomas promise to send me North, and never to breathe a word. If she lives, why would she destroy her notion of respectability and the family name by letting the truth come out here in South Carolina?"

"Well, we could at least try. You're more an Elwood than Emma ever was."

"In her eyes, and doubtless Clarissa's too, I'm a monster. The reason Emma's son, Jefferson, died."

"But he raped you."

"And? No one cared if a colored woman was raped just like no one cares if it happens now. That Thomas should have killed his stepbrother in a duel over it, is to her a clear sign of insanity."

"So you're just gonna give in without a fight? Hand over all this to her?"

"No. I'll attend the hearing and put my case. But justice doesn't apply to us, you know that. It'll take divine intervention for the judge to take my side."

"We'll be ruined then."

"No, we'll figure something out. That's what everyone else has to do. Joshua, there's something I've been meaning to tell you, but recent events have been so awful I decided to wait."

"What now?"

"Don't look so concerned. This time it's wonderful news."

"Wonderful?"

"Exactly. I wasn't sure at first but now I am. We have a baby on the way."

"Oh, Mosa, that is wonderful news," said Joshua hugging her.

The court building in Columbia had been destroyed, and the new one was still under construction.

The hearing took place in the open under a tarpaulin hidden from the street by the wall of a building, the rest of which had been gutted by the attack on the capital of the State.

In the empty space, three tables had been arranged. One at the front for the judge, facing the other two which were positioned side by side.

Emma and her lawyer were already sitting behind one when Mosa and Joshua arrived. Emma glanced only briefly at Mosa, giving her a look of thinly disguised disgust, narrowing her eyes and wrinkling her nose as if they smelled unpleasant.

Emma had dressed in grand style. She wore a pale mauve dress of high quality fabric with a large silver brooch and a matching hat, perched like a bird's nest on her head. The contrast with Mosa's tired plain brown dress couldn't have been greater. Yet another reason for the judge to rule in Emma's favor. After all, how could someone who looked as impecunious as Mosa be trusted by the likes of him. No one would know that Emma had spent every last cent she had to acquire her outfit.

All four and the court clerk stood as the white judge appeared.

"Be seated. I have read the petitioner's deposition so unless there is anything Mrs. Emma Elwood wishes to add I shall be interested to hear from Mosa Elwood."

"There is nothing more, thank you your Honor," responded Emma's pretend attorney, his tone as gooey as mud from a swamp.

"Miss Mosa Elwood."

"Your Honor." Mosa coughed as she stood up from

her chair in an attempt to conceal the nervousness in her voice. The confidence that she had acquired from speaking in front of a room of school
children had deserted her when confronted by the
stern stare of the judge. "I was born to Jane Elwood
and George Elwood on their plantation. I later
discovered through Thomas, their son and my
brother, that our father's great great grandfather
was an African which accounts for my skin color.

"My father disowned me and I was brought up
as a slave on another plantation. I only found
out about my parentage when I was older from
Thomas who had unearthed the truth.

"To keep my birth a secret, George Elwood had his
wife, Jane, confined to an asylum where she eventually became insane. Even though his wife was
still alive, albeit under another name, he went
ahead and married Emma."

Mosa glanced in Emma's direction as she said this.
The look of astonishment on the woman's face
indicated that she hadn't known about Jane not
being dead.

"When our father died, Thomas inherited the
plantation. When he himself died, being the kind
and loving brother he was, he bequeathed it to
me."

"Well, I can see you're definitely not pure Negro.
But because you're a mulatto doesn't establish
that your parents were both white and George
Elwood, the epitome of a Southern gentleman, a
bigamist. Is there anyone of respectable charac-

ter who could confirm your rather sensational account?"

"Maisie, a former slave who was present at my birth, witnessed it with her very own eyes. She's waiting outside and ready to give evidence."

"That won't be necessary."

"But your Honor-"

"No, she would not be a suitable witness. Mr. Jamieson, do you have any questions for Mosa Elwood?"

Jamieson stood, removing the small round eyeglasses perched on the end of his long, thin nose.

"No, your Honor. Her fanciful story, for that is all it is, speaks for itself. It would make a wonderfully entertaining novel but it isn't grounded in reality."

"Indeed, in the absence of any corroboration I am not convinced. I am inclined to agree that no right-thinking man of sound mind would leave such wealth to a slave gal. However, I shall give the matter further consideration, and we shall reconvene here at the same time next week when I shall give my ruling. This court is adjourned."

Joshua, Mosa, and Maisie exchanged few words on the way home. A black person might now be able to put their case in court, but the chances of their word being believed were practically nonexistent. It was abundantly clear to them how the judge was intending to rule.

Mosa fretted about what would happen to the other families. Would Emma require them to leave and turn them into vagrants, making them effectively slave labor once more? She hoped the woman would at least offer them work, albeit that the wages would almost certainly be derisory. Perhaps she would sell the plantation. Emma wasn't the type who enjoyed that kind of life. She could pocket the money and return to Charleston to pursue a life of dinner parties and nights out at the theater.

Mosa got her answer when they arrived back. As they turned off the road, Gregory Brown was waiting for them.

"How'd it go today?"

"How do you know about it?" asked Mosa.

"The late George Elwood's wife has been in correspondence with me. Anyway, you don't have to answer my question, I can tell from your expression that it mustn't have gone well for you. You should have sold the plantation to me when you had the chance. Now she'll get all that money when I buy it. She's only made one condition. That I don't let you stay here."

He gave a smile that reeked of insincerity before riding off.

CHAPTER 7

"I think we should tell everybody else," said Mosa. "Give them time to prepare for what's coming."

"Prepare for what?" asked Joshua.

"Decide what they want to do."

"Well if Brown's buying it, they can be sharecroppers. Let's wait till morning. I'm dead beat."

When Mosa awoke the next day, Joshua was already up. She found him saddling Shadow.

"Where are you going?"

"I'm gonna ride down to Charleston and find Clarissa if she's still alive."

"Like I've already explained, she's not gonna help us."

"Maybe not but it's got to be worth a try."

"Is it? It's dangerous out there. Going all that way alone. Our baby needs a father more than he needs a plantation."

"Look, I don't want any child of mine growing up a slave in all but name, tied to somebody else's land. Making them money and being dirt poor all his life. I'll be OK. You took plenty of risks coming down here from New York and you made it. I'll be back in a few days. Now give me a kiss."

Mosa watched him go until he was out of sight. She would try not to but she knew she would be worrying every day until he got back. Later that morning, she gave the news of the court case to the other families.

"Well, now we know," said one of the men. "We've always been wondering why Thomas would've left you the land."

"Will you be staying?" asked one of the women.

"I don't suppose so. I expect me, Joshua, and his Mama will seek our fortune elsewhere."

"Well, good luck to you. You deserve it."

After four days, Mosa's unease intensified. Joshua should have been back already. She didn't say anything but she could see it in Maisie's eyes too.

It wasn't until late in the day before the hearing that he returned. Mosa went running down the track toward him. Getting down off his horse, he embraced her.

"Joshua, don't ever do this to me again. I thought you were never coming back."

"Neither did I. I got picked up in Charleston. They said without a written contract on me, I couldn't prove I was employed. They wouldn't believe that anyone like us could own land. I managed to escape at night and luckily Shadow was still tethered outside."

"See I told you, you should never have gone. Don't suppose-"

"No. I found out where she lived but she died a

few weeks ago. I think we should try going North. Once you lose the land and we're kicked out, I wouldn't be surprised if they take me in again if we stay, and hire me out as free labor."

"We'd probably get arrested traveling North. They're saying now you can't enter another State in the South without getting someone to post a bond for your good behavior. Maybe Brown would let us work on his land. He only said that Emma required him not to let us stay here. I'll go visit him after I fix you some dinner."

"OK, we can do that while we try to think of something better. Don't worry about feeding me. I'll ask Mama."

"She ain't here."

"Ain't here? Where'd she go?"

"Got Jobe to ride her into town first thing apparently. Left word she'd see us there in the morning. Said there was someone she wanted to visit."

Mosa felt glum as she walked up to Gregory Brown's mansion. She had never expected to be walking this way again. She had always thought that part of her life was behind her.

Yet instead her life had gone full circle. She'd been brought here as a baby and worked picking cotton until she had been transferred to the Old Oaks Plantation after saving Thomas from drowning. Now she would be pleading for Brown to take her back, to let her and her husband, and any children of theirs just as soon as they were old enough, toil in the fields all day to keep him rich and them poor.

He was sitting on his veranda but stood and descended the steps from the house when he saw her coming up the path.

"What brings you here? I already told you, it's too late to sell the plantation to me."

"You mentioned that Emma Elwood would require me to leave. I've come to ask if that applies to your plantation also."

"It does not."

"In that case, I wanted to ask if you would be willing to consider taking on me and my husband, Joshua. We're both hard workers."

"Well, I could do with some more hands. Many of my niggers fled during the war or have gone died of disease. You'll have to sign a contract. You and your husband can come over the day after tomorrow to do that. The day after the ruling. Emma's told me it's tomorrow.

"You know, the funny thing is I think you're telling the truth. I asked around those who've been here many years. They told me you were brought here as a newborn, which don't make sense. George Elwood was as miserly as they come, and if he'd fathered a slave girl he would have kept her to work her when she grew older, that's for damn sure. Kept her unless there was something he needed to hide. And I was aware Jane Elwood was brought back from Charleston by you, as crazy as they come by all accounts."

"Oh, Mr. Brown, could you not come tomorrow

and tell the judge? Please, sir."

"Why would I want to do that and lose my deal. Anyhow, me just repeating what my niggers told me ain't evidence. Now you run along and I'll see you the day after tomorrow. Make sure you and that husband of yours are here before noon or my offer will be withdrawn."

He returned to the veranda. Mosa walked slowly back, fighting to hold in tears of frustration.

The next morning, it was raining heavily as she and Joshua rode the cart into Columbia. By the time they arrived the storm had passed but they were soaked through, looking bedraggled and defeated.

Their low spirits were raised to see Maisie waiting for them. They had feared for her safety. They were, however, curious as to why an elderly white man, stooped and leaning on his cane, should be standing at her side.

CHAPTER 8

"This here is Dr. Brown. He was there at your birth," explained Maisie.

Mosa's expression was one of confusion.

"I don't understand."

"Maisie told me what's happened. I wasn't inclined to help initially but she's a persuasive character. Made me see that I couldn't bring any shame to Mr. and Mrs. Elwood, given they are both dead, and I don't like to see such an injustice as is about to occur."

"So you'll give evidence for us?"

"Well, I'm not standing here for the good of my health."

Mosa and Joshua smiled at each other. At last there was hope.

"Dr. Brown, what a pleasant surprise to see you as always. But what are you doing in my courtroom if this poor excuse for one can be called such?"

"Your Honor," said Mosa. "You explained last time that you wanted corroboration, which Dr. Brown is here to provide."

The judge raised his eyebrows at Dr. Brown seeking confirmation, which he gave with a brief nod.

"Take the stand Doctor."

After the oath was administered, the judge invited Mosa to question him.

"Dr. Brown could you describe the birth please."

"It was about twenty-five years ago. I was at the Elwood's property to deliver Jane Elwood's child. The baby born to her was a girl. Her skin color was a light brown, a half and half. George Elwood was naturally unhappy, and accused his wife of having had carnal relations with a Negro. She resolutely denied it. I did advise him that I'd heard of rare cases where the color of an ancestor could surface generations later. He was furious and wanted to cover it all up, mortified as to what people would think if they found out."

"Thank you, Doctor."

"Mr. Jamieson, do you have questions for the witness?"

Both Emma and the law clerk had been in a state of disbelief since Mosa had announced she had a witness. Jamieson appeared lost for words. Emma nudged him hard with her elbow.

"Do something." Her whisper was loud.

"Er...yes. Yes, I do."

He fumbled with the papers which he had strewn on the table in front of him as he played for time, desperately trying to think of the questions he should ask. The judge became impatient.

"Well, Mr. Jamieson? I can't leave Dr. Brown stuck on the witness stand all day."

Jamieson smiled inwardly. Inspiration had come to him at last. He felt his confidence growing as he got up and approached the doctor. He was good at this. Once they had the money from the sale of the land, he would study to be a lawyer. He would make a good one. At last a master, no more a servant, no longer somebody's clerk to be pushed around.

"Dr. Brown, how do you know Mrs. Elwood hadn't given birth to a Negro's child?"

"I knew her well. She was a very respectable lady. I really think that very unlikely."

"But you don't know for certain, do you? It's not a fact which you can swear is true."

"No, I can't."

"And even if the child was the result of the union between Mr. and Mrs. Elwood, how do you know that Mosa Elwood here is the one, and not just some grifter who acquired knowledge of the event and is seeking to take advantage of it?"

"Well, she is the right age."

"So are many former slave girls. Can you confirm that she's the one? The one you delivered so many years ago."

"I believe she is but no, I can't give a hundred percent guarantee."

"With respect Doctor, you can't give even a ten percent guarantee. I have no further questions for the witness, your Honor."

"Thank you Dr. Brown. You may step down."

Emma smiled at Jamieson as he returned to sit

down next to her. He leaned back in his chair and folded his arms in satisfaction. Mosa hadn't proved anything. It was all just speculation.

"I shall now proceed to give my ruling," said the judge. "I certainly find Dr. Brown a reliable and credible witness. I therefore find that Mrs. Jane Elwood did indeed give birth to a mulatto. One can engage in sordid speculation as to who the father might be, but even if the late Mrs. Elwood had behaved completely out of character, her child would still have been the half sister of Thomas Elwood.

"Leaving one's estate to a sister or a half-sister is not evidence of an unsound mind. The crucial question therefore is whether Mosa Elwood is that person."

Mosa felt as though the world had come to a halt. The judge had stopped talking, he rankled the end of his nose and pushed his lips out as he engaged in contemplation. Their future hung by a thread, one which he could so easily cut with what he had to say next.

To him, the very presence of black people in a courtroom, other than defendants in criminal cases where a guilty verdict would have been a foregone conclusion, must have seemed surreal. Yet another unwelcome change to the Southern way of life which he and so many others had enjoyed for generations. Mosa thought it unlikely that he was capable of ignoring her color and considering the matter dispassionately. A man who had spent his life upholding a system that dispensed justice according to race.

"The standard required in this case is proof by preponderance of the evidence." His arcane language and a long pause seemed to confirm her expectation. "In this case that standard has not been reached. It is for your client, Mr. Jamieson, to prove that Mr. Thomas Elwood was of unsound mine and if he was not, that Mosa Elwood here is not who she says she is. I have found that Mr. Elwood was not of unsound mind when he made his bequest, and I further find that the woman before us is his sister. Your client's motion is therefore denied. This matter is closed."

As he brought down his gavel firmly on his table, both Mosa and Maisie covered their mouths with their hands in a mixture of surprise and relief before hugging each other.

Emma was unable to hide her fury, turning upon the hapless law clerk who she had tolerated for so long only because she believed that he would get her the plantation.

"I knew I should've gotten me a proper attorney. I'm going back to Charleston, and don't even think about coming to look for me."

She flounced out.

"Dearest Maisie," said Mosa as she withdrew from her embrace. "I'm in your debt once again. First you save my life and now you save our land, our very future. How can I ever repay you?"

"By giving me a grandson," she said putting her

hand on Mosa's stomach.

"It might well be a girl."

"Either will be a blessed gift."

As their horse and cart reached Old Oaks Plantation, they encountered Gregory Brown.

"I've just been over to speak to your people to explain how things will work here in future. Don't forget to be on time tomorrow."

"We appreciate your offer," said Joshua, "but we won't be coming."

"Suit yourself, but you won't find anything better. The sale should close next week so make sure you're off the property by then, or I'll send my men round. Shooting trespassers is no crime."

"There won't be no sale. The judge ruled in our favor."

The expression on Brown's face which began as one of incredulity soon became one of barely concealed anger.

"Are you telling me that even our judiciary is controlled by the goddamn Yankees now? I can see you're mighty pleased with yourself, but one of these days your luck is gonna run out, and when it does don't come looking to me for any favors. Huh!"

He kicked his horse hard in its side and departed at speed.

"My, we sure made him mad," laughed Mosa.

CHAPTER 9

Subdued by Gregory Brown's visit, it was a somber crowd which awaited their arrival. When Mosa gave them the news, they erupted with delight. There was unanimous agreement to Joshua's suggestion that there be a hog roast that evening to celebrate.

When all had eaten their fill, Joshua stood up and called for attention.

"Mosa and I talked about the future on the way back. None of us are achieving anything, tilling a small piece of ground. As most of you must know by now, the government has ruled that all land be returned to the original owners. We don't mean to be greedy but if we're all gonna have a better life, we need to do something different to what we're already doing. This land is Mosa's.

"We're intending to seek a bank loan so we can buy some cottonseed and other things we'll need to start growing again. There's currently a cotton shortage with the collapse in production as a result of the war so we should be able to make a good profit. A profit we'll share with each one of you, after setting aside enough to buy supplies for the following year. And it'll be a whole lot more than you could make any place else. Any questions?

There was complete silence.

"Well, as there don't appear to be any objections, do I have your agreement?"

Nodding heads confirmed their assent.

Neither Joshua nor Mosa had ever entered a bank before. It was a strange world to them. Men behind desks. Piles of paper. Hushed voices. There was almost a sense of reverence. A place so solemn and joyless as if it were some kind of white man's church, thought Mosa. An officious man accosted them.

"What are you doing in here? Be off with you. Get out of here. Go."

"We've come to see about a bank loan."

Both were wearing their best clothes, hoping to convey a good impression.

"You should speak to your master. He'll organize credit through his connections. We don't lend to farm laborers, even if you have dressed up for the occasion."

"We don't have a master. We own a plantation. It was bequeathed to my wife here. We wish to borrow so it can produce cotton again."

"Is that right." The man began to show some interest. Perhaps there was money to be made. "Follow me." He led them to one of the desks. "You may sit. I'll need some details."

They answered his questions and he wrote their

answers on a form, assuming that neither could read or write.

"I'll need to clear this with my manager. If he approves, someone will come out to appraise the land, and should we think it is a suitable proposition, the bank will make you an offer. It'll require a mortgage on the property and should you for any reason default on the loan, the bank will foreclose and you will lose the property."

"We understand," said Joshua.

"Good, we'll be in touch if we wish to take this further. You can go now."

The man casually pushed his hand into the air toward them to dismiss them. He saw no need to be courteous to such people. As they made their way out, they could sense all eyes were upon them and they could overhear the conversation taking place behind their backs.

"What was that all about?"

"Niggers who own a plantation."

"Well, I'll be damned. Whatever next?"

Weeks passed and they heard nothing. There was good news, however. In the mid-term Congressional elections of 1866, so-called Radical Republicans took control. Incensed at the way in which President Johnson had allowed the Southern States to pay only lip service to the ending of slavery so that a new system could be created to achieve a similar outcome, they were determined to push for more equal rights. Mosa, Joshua, and millions like them waited hopefully for a change to come in 1867 when the new Congressmen would take their seats.

There was more good news for them that year. Their child was born. Joshua had tears streaming down his face the first time he held the boy. When his first wife and child had died, the prospect of a family had seemed something that would elude him for always.

"Isn't he beautiful," said Mosa as she lay in bed resting while Joshua cuddled their son. "And what's best of all, he's born free. I know it's far from a perfect freedom, but with all that's happening I truly believe times are a changing, changing for the better."

Maisie was ecstatic about her first grandchild. The ever-present melancholy, which had wrapped itself tightly around her like a vine strangling a tree since Jacob's murder, released its grip.

"What will you call him?"

"Thomas Jacob," said Mosa.

"That's a good name for you to have my little one. They were both good, fine men."

Late one morning not long after the birth, those on the plantation heard again the sound that seemed so often to be a harbinger of doom. Horses' hooves. All looked up from their work to see three white men approaching. Never had the arrival of that race brought them good news.

CHAPTER 10

They were soldiers and their demeanor was friendly.

"We've come to enroll the men as voters."

"Voters?" asked Joshua in disbelief.

The constitution that the State had adopted after the war hadn't included giving black people the vote. That was a step too far for the white population, still reeling with bitterness at the ending of slavery. With a third of all white men of military service age in South Carolina dead from the conflict, it would have handed control of the State government to those who had until recently been only property.

Able to override President Johnson's veto, the new Congress had passed the Reconstruction Acts, placing Southern States under the direct control of the United States Army in response to the refusal of those States to grant equal rights and recognize African Americans as citizens.

"Yes, every man over the age of twenty-one, regardless of color, is to be permitted to vote for delegates to a State Convention which will adopt a new constitution. Are you the one in charge here?"

"Me and my wife own the plantation, yes."

"You might like to consider standing as a delegate yourself. You should visit the Republican Party offices in Columbia. They're keen to put men such as you on the ballot."

"I don't know about that."

"Oh Joshua, you must," said Mosa squeezing his arm. "This is the chance of a lifetime. Think of what you could do for us, for everyone. You could help create a Constitution where all are equal."

"Yes son, think how proud your father up in Heaven will be. You'll be doing something he couldn't even have dreamed of," added Maisie.

"Well, maybe I'll go inquire."

"You could argue for women to get the vote too," said Mosa.

"You're joking right?"

Mosa shook her head with weary resignation. Nonetheless it was a profoundly moving sight to see the men line up to register to vote. True liberty it seemed was finally coming to this land, albeit women, whatever their color, would continue to be ignored.

Joshua did stand for election and along with seventy-four other black men was elected, compared with only forty-eight white men. In early 1868, they spent two months in Charleston debating and finally agreeing upon a new Constitution. Joshua could still hardly believe what was happening when he woke up each morning. He, until recently a slave, was helping to determine the way in which the State would henceforth be governed. Outraged that all men were given the right to vote, the white population sought to prevent the new Constitution taking effect by almost unanimously boycotting the vote to ratify it. To be adopted, it was required to be voted for by a majority of all registered voters. Although the vote was close, the larger black vote carried the day. At the same time, representatives were elected to the US Congress and to the State Legislature, including Joshua. It was the first ever State Legislature to have a majority of black Representatives, a beautiful irony given that South Carolina had been the first State to secede from the United States to avoid any restrictions on slavery.

Mosa's face was radiant with joy when she attended the inauguration in Columbia to watch Joshua being sworn in. The roof of the State House was still only temporarily covered and flapped noisily in the wind, and the holes from shells fired by Sherman's men were clearly visible. Nonetheless it remained an impressive building, and a place she could finally be proud of. No longer one where white supremacists would gather to pass laws to keep half the population downtrodden and impoverished.

Yet in reality, prejudice was still embedded in people's minds as much as bullets in a body and the new liberties had only shallow roots, dependent on the presence of the army. The Ku Klux Klan had established itself across the South, terrorizing black people and those few whites who supported the new order. Mosa's happiness was tinged with fear, a fear that like his brother, Joshua would now be a target. He wouldn't be the first Republican politician in the South to be attacked if he were.

However, Joshua felt safe enough in the State capital and found great satisfaction in his new career. He immersed himself in every opportunity which presented itself, getting involved in matters as diverse as establishing a public education system for all and the Bills to authorize railroad construction to replace those destroyed in the conflict.

Joshua also enjoyed the camaraderie of his colleagues. The endless dinners and the drinking. It was all new to him and he liked it. After a lifetime where the plantation had been the limit of his horizons, he wanted to make up for lost time, to seize the possibilities in case like a rainbow it should all suddenly disappear.

Joshua decided to visit the bank again. This time, once he had identified himself as a legislator, he was treated as if he were white. It wasn't long after that until a bank official went out to assess the property. An offer of a loan was made.

They were able to replant the plantation with cotton. Though the work was every bit as hard as when they had been enslaved, this time they weren't working to enrich somebody else and their efforts would be rewarded. Each day, Mosa joined the others with baby Thomas tied to her back.

Most of the time Joshua had to be in Columbia, and usually only returned to Old Oaks when the Legislature wasn't sitting.

One morning as he strolled toward it, he heard a woman across the street call his name. He watched her as she made her way across, navigating past horses and carriages. She looked familiar yet different. Her style was more sophisticated than when he had known her. Her hair was up in a chignon and she wore a green dress and hat to match which complemented her pale emerald eyes.

"Lowenna?"

"Joshua. What are you doing here?"

"I was elected to office so I live here most of the time. We were worried about you. Mosa will be relieved to know you are all right."

"Indeed I am. I'm sorry that I didn't write. I should have."

"Well, we all have busy lives. Are you living in town?"

"Yes."

"I have to go now, but perhaps we could meet for a coffee and catch up on all the news. Mosa will be annoyed if I don't get all the details."

Lowenna laughed.

"We women just like to keep up with what's going on. Yes, I would like that."

"How about O'Leary's coffee house on Saturday at

ten?"

CHAPTER 11

Even in this new regime the races mixed rarely. The majority of white people refused to frequent establishments that allowed black customers. O' Leary's was one of the few that welcomed anyone. As such it had become a favorite haunt of the Republican Representatives as well as carpetbaggers, those Northerners who had come South to help fight for equality, and scallywags, the minority of Southerners who supported the idea.

Lowenna was already seated when Joshua arrived. The rich smell of coffee and her smile were enticing.

"You look so different from when last I saw you. A real man about town," she commented.

"And you look like a lady of high society. What do you do here?"

"Not a great deal. I do some charity work, helping out at the hospital mainly. I remarried."

"Congratulations. And who is the lucky man?"

"Thackeray Gillingham."

"Is he a Republican?"

"No, a Democrat through and through. He fought

65

for the Confederacy."

"Oh."

"Please don't think badly of me. I was destitute and alone. I needed my boy to be safe."

"You don't love him then?"

"Women can't always marry for love. He takes care of me and Abe. Anyway, enough about me. How is Mosa?"

"Real good. We have a son, Thomas, and another baby on the way. Mosa's hoping for a girl. I don't get to see them as much as I would like. My work keeps me here most of the time."

"Do give her my best wishes. I should leave now. As you can imagine, if my husband knew I was here, he wouldn't be happy. But I wanted to have the chance to thank you, thank you both for taking care of me and Abe."

"It was our pleasure."

Joshua watched her leave. Mosa would be disappointed that she hadn't got to see her. He was disappointed too. He missed a woman's company. All his days and evenings were spent with men, save for the rare times when he was able to go home.

On the plantation later that day, Mosa sat in a rocking chair enjoying the evening sun. Joshua had brought it for her on one of his visits. As she rocked, she rubbed her bump in a circular motion.

"I'd say by the shape of you, the baby's gonna be a girl," said Maisie as she sat in a chair beside her, bouncing Thomas on her knees.

"I'll be glad when it's born whatever it is. Being

pregnant and this hot weather don't go together."

"Well, you should follow my advice and not come to work in the fields. We ain't slaves no more. You don't have to be out there."

"It'll be cotton picking time soon. All hands will be needed."

"We got plenty of hands. You not being there ain't gonna matter one bit."

"Guess I'm just worried about anything going wrong. We need that crop to come in good to pay the bank."

"It will, and you fretting about it is just a waste of your time and will upset the baby."

Mosa did worry. Worry about more than just the cotton. Since Joshua had been elected and was making money for the first time in his life, he was spending a lot, always buying new things. Not that he wasn't generous. For every fine garment which he bought for himself, she had a new dress or piece of jewelry. She thought of how they had argued the last time he came home.

"Are those more new clothes you're wearing?" Mosa had asked as he arrived.

"Yes, do you like them? They're from France. Wait there, I have something for you tied to my horse. Close your eyes."

When he returned, she felt the weight of a box in her arms.

"Open your eyes now and have a look inside."

She laid it on the bed and lifted off the lid. It was an expensive looking yellow dress.

"Well, do you like it? The lady in the store said it's the very latest design from New York."

"It's lovely, but..."

"But what?"

"When am I ever gonna get the chance to wear it?" The other plantation owners in the county weren't going to be inviting them to their parties. They saw the couple as an unwelcome reminder of all that had been taken away from them. That their workers would get to share in their success rubbed salt in the wound, and made the other owners concerned those on their own plantations might rise up and demand better treatment.

"You can wear it to the Governor's ball."

"But I already have the one you brought last time. Are you sure we're not spending too much? Shouldn't we be putting some aside for a rainy day?"

"Why can't you just be grateful, Mosa. I'm working my ass off to make the money for these things."

"I know you are but so am I. While you're out partying, I'm here trying to hold it all together. And this place needs some work since last year's storms. You've never bothered fixing it."

"I've got a better idea. I'm having plans drawn up for a new house to replace the one that got burned down in the fire. You won't be living in a stick house no more. You'll have a mansion."

"Really. And how are we gonna pay for that? Have you forgotten how much we already owe the bank?"

"It's time to start thinking like the Americans we now are. Think small and you'll still be bringing up our family in this place in five years time. You don't get rich that way. The bank will make us another loan. We can pay it off with next year's crop. You gotta stop thinking like a slave."

"Thinking like a slave? My, you sure have some nerve. I need some air. And when you leave you can take that dress with you, I don't want it."

Mosa was proud of all Joshua had achieved. After all, it had been she who had encouraged him to make a career in politics. However, she feared they were drifting apart. Their lives were now so different and spent mainly separated.

Joshua spoke so enthusiastically of the fine meals and wine he consumed that she felt embarrassment at the very ordinary food which she had to feed him when he visited. She must come across as dull to him. While he had stories of rebuilding and progress, of interesting people he had met, Mosa had nothing to talk of but the same old people and how the cotton was growing.

He was coming home even less than previously. The last trip he had canceled. Apparently he'd had to go down to Charleston for a meeting. There was even talk of a visit to Washington. He would be gone for weeks if that went ahead.

In bed that night Mosa tossed and turned, her mind twirling and unable to find a comfortable position to sleep in. It was late when she finally fell asleep.

Shouting awoke her. It was still dark. In only her nightdress, she went outside. Others were up already, running around in a state of commotion. Some ran past her with buckets, water slopping out as they did so. An orange glow lit the sky.

Mosa hurried past the huts which blocked her view. The sight which greeted her was her worst nightmare. Many of the cotton bushes were alight, and the fire was spreading fast along the neat rows which they had planted with such care.

She could see straight away that it was hopeless. The fire had too good a hold. Cinders flew about in the air like little devils. One landed on her face. Even though she brushed it off quickly, she felt it burn.

Transfixed by the destruction she didn't move, watching in silent horror as the entire crop turned to ash. Come dawn the sorry picture was fully revealed. What had yesterday been so bountiful, smoldered, the promise it held devoured as if the crop had been savaged by a plague of fire breathing locusts.

Mosa shed no tears. She was too overwhelmed to cry and it wouldn't alter anything.

There was no conversation. Weary and dejected, families returned to their huts to get some rest. Mosa remained, staring at the apocalyptic scene. This had surely been no accident. It had to be the work of those who hated them and didn't want them to be here. Gregory Brown was probably involved, but she would never be able to prove that it was arson and who had done it.

"Come." Maisie appeared, putting her arm around her shoulder. "There's nothing more that can be done. Let me fix you some breakfast."

"I'm not hungry."

"You need to eat, keep your strength up for the baby."

Mosa didn't resist and followed her mother-in-law back.

CHAPTER 12

That evening, Lowenna and her husband sat eating their dinner in silence. They nearly always did. They no longer knew what to say to each other, not that theirs had been a talkative relationship even at the start.

She had met Thackery Gillingham soon after coming to Columbia. She had been frightened and vulnerable, traumatized by that awful night when she had been forced to leave the plantation.

As they had ridden, she had put her hands over her son's ears to cover the screams of pain coming from Jacob as he was dragged along like nothing more than a sack of potatoes. Their horse had been sent on ahead, but she'd still been able to hear him pleading in vain for his life.

When the others caught up with them, the leader gave her a warning.

"Don't ever speak of what happened tonight. I'd hate to see any harm come to your boy."

Once they'd reached Columbia, they had left her and her son and rode off into the night. Come morning, she went looking for work. She found a job at the hospital and got an advance so that they could rent a room to live in.

Thackery chaired the board of governors and their paths soon crossed. He'd seemed pleasant enough. With his full, round face, white hair, whiskers and beard, he could have passed for Santa Clause if he had been of a jollier disposition.

She had accepted his invitations to dine. Even though he was older than her own father would have been, she also accepted his proposal of marriage. Lowenna calculated that his age would be an advantage, his demands less frequent, and there was the promise of an inheritance when he died.

They lived a comfortable life with a cook and a housemaid to take care of them. Her husband passed his days with his former brothers in arms. Lowenna had found safety for her son. The price was boredom. She dabbled in the odd charitable cause, though found the company of Southern ladies less than fulfilling. Often she wondered how different her life might have been if she had never come South. Yet that was just idle speculation. As her mother would most certainly have told her, "You've made your bed, so lie in it."

Lowenna envied Mosa. Joshua was a man a woman could be proud of. A man for the future, not one wedded to the past, always complaining that the country had gone to hell in a handbasket.

Lloyd had been a man Lowenna was proud of. A man of ideals and enthusiastic for change.

Lowenna learned patience, not something that

she had ever previously been good at. Time seemed to pass at a glacial pace here in South Carolina. One day, she tried to convince herself, something would change that would make her one-dimensional world more exciting.

"I have some old pals coming round. I'll see you in the morning," said her husband, pushing his chair back and standing up from the dining table.

As usual Lowenna would retire to her bedroom to read or embroider. She was glad that he preferred having his own room and came to visit her increasingly rarely. Looking in on her son, she planted a kiss on his forehead as he slept.

It was an unpleasantly warm night. Like the effect on the throat from a sip of cognac, the air in her nostrils felt hot each time she took a breath. Through her open window she heard the arrival of her husband's guests.

She reached out for the water jug on the stand next to her to pour a glass. It was empty. Rather than ring the bell and disturb the housemaid, Lowenna decided she would go downstairs to the kitchen herself.

Her route there took her past the parlor. Though the door was closed, low conspiratorial voices caught her attention. She halted, curious as to what they might be discussing.

"He told me a bunch of them are gathering tomorrow night on the edge of town for a picnic. There won't be any army around to protect them."

"Exactly, we mount a raid at dusk and disappear

long before any help arrives. A few dead Republican legislators will the make the rest think very carefully about their position."

Lowenna had heard enough. Passing through the kitchen, she abandoned the water jug and went out through the back door.

She made her way across town. Her agitation sped her on. Her thumping heart wasn't so much from the exertion but from revulsion at who she had married, revulsion and the fear of discovery.

Lowenna had always known Thackeray was committed to the Old South, but never had she considered he would be part of the insurgency. Now she knew that she was tied to a man who would kill, and doubtless had before, those who espoused equality. A man who would probably kill her if he knew what she was doing. Maybe he'd even been part of the mob that had murdered Jacob.

She arrived at the house. Fortunately, he'd mentioned where he lived. There was faint candlelight coming from the second floor. She knocked, quietly at first. Getting no response, she knocked more loudly, all the while concerned the noise would attract someone's attention. From a door or a window, a person might see her. Recognize her and let her husband know she had been there. To his house.

The door opened a little and a pair of eyes peered through the gap.

"Lowenna, what are you doing here?"

"Let me in. Quick, before I am seen."

As he opened the door fully, he let his right arm drop and laid the pistol which he had been holding on the hall table.

"A precaution. You never know, especially at night."

"You and your colleagues are in danger. I heard men talking tonight at our house. They sound like they're Klan members. Said they were going to attack the Republican gathering tomorrow evening."

"Thank you. I was going to be there myself. You've done good."

"I should be going."

"No, stay a while. Please."

Joshua placed his hand on her shoulder. Lowenna felt a warmth inside, a yearning. A yearning for tenderness. Something to make her feel alive, not suffocated.

He sensed that too in the way she looked at him. No words were exchanged, but their eyes spoke. He leaned toward her and placed his lips on hers. She didn't resist his kiss. Her lips opened.

When Joshua moved his mouth away from hers and offered her his hand, she accepted. He led her up the staircase.

"You shouldn't be going. Not in your condition," Maisie had told Mosa earlier that evening. "Let one of the men go tell him about the fire."

"No, I want to. I have to talk to him. Discuss what we should do."

"At least let someone accompany you."

"There's no need. I'll take the cart. I can stay the night and rest. You'll watch Thomas for me, won't you."

Now it was night. Ahead she could see the silhouettes of the buildings. She was almost there. Mosa hadn't seen the house he now rented, but he'd described where it was. She hadn't understood why he needed a whole house for just one person. He would need to go back to renting only a room to save money. If the bank agreed to extend the loan, they'd surely insist that they kept their expenditure to a minimum. That is if they would extend the loan. Mosa was clinging to the hope that they would.

A soft glow shone through the drapes upstairs. Good, Joshua was still awake.

CHAPTER 13

Mosa tried the front door. It opened. She ascended the stairs. His bedroom door was ajar.

Shadows danced on the wall opposite. Two shadows, moving in unison. Moving with passion. How embarrassing, thought Mosa. I've entered the wrong house. She went to go, but a woman's voice saying her husband's name forced her to accept that her attempt at self-deception was useless.

A wave of nausea hit Mosa. She put her hand on the wall to steady herself, her mind spinning in a frenzy. Then instinct kicked in. She flung the door right open and walked into the room.

"What on earth is going on here?"

The flush of pleasure on Joshua's face was washed away by the shock. Lowenna pulled the sheets onto her chest, her head down with shame.

"Lowenna? How could you. And you, Joshua."

Tears stung her eyes. Mosa held them back as she swiftly descended the staircase, ignoring Joshua's pleas to wait. Once back on the cart and in motion, she let those tears escape.

Mosa had but one focus, to get away from there.

She drove the horse fast, too fast. Every bump jolted her, threatened to turn the cart on its side. Mosa didn't care.

Not far out of the town a sudden sharp pain shot through her, causing her to lurch forward in agony. She slowed down. She mustn't endanger her baby.

It came again, like a knife whose owner was twisting it for maximum effect. She must get back. Get back before the child was born.

Mosa felt liquid between her legs. She didn't need to look to know.

Light was breaking as she returned. Maisie was already up and helped her down and into the cabin. A neighbor took Thomas away as he bawled for his Mama.

"Hush. You'll get to see your new brother or sister soon enough. While we wait, I'm gonna cook you the best breakfast you ever had."

Maisie got Mosa to lie down. It was too soon for the child to be born. Maisie fought to conceal her concern but acting wasn't something she did well. Her furrowed brow was an open book.

Later that day, Mosa had a girl. She named her Martha after her friend at the orphanage in New York where she had worked.

Martha never cried as newborn babies do. After Mosa had held her for a while, Maisie gently took her from Mosa's arms. That was the last she ever saw of her child.

Joshua arrived just in time to see his mother carrying the little bundle toward a group that had gathered around the freshly dug earth. He raced into the cabin and sank to his knees beside the bed.

"I'm so sorry, Mosa. So sorry." Sobs threatened to choke off his words. "Please forgive me."

"There was a fire. We lost the crop. You need to go. Go back. Go see the bank and ask for an extension to the loan."

Her voice was detached, devoid of emotion. She turned away from him and faced the wall. Her heart was heavier than a lead weight. If only she had heeded Maisie's advice and hadn't gone to see him.

At first the wretchedness of her guilt was overwhelming, submerging her in a whirlpool of blame. Yet as she repeatedly replayed events in her mind, her mood began to change. It wasn't really her fault. She was going to spend the night in Columbia. She would have spent the night there. None of this would have happened if her husband hadn't betrayed her. This was his doing, not hers.

Joshua visited the bank. They agreed to extend the loan and advance some more for new seed and supplies. There would be default interest and compound interest to pay in addition, and a higher rate of interest for the new loan for the greater risk, the manager explained. Joshua didn't follow all these terms. When she got the letter, Mosa did. It would be some years until they had paid it all off. Still, better that than the bank foreclose on them. She signed.

The land hadn't mattered quite so much before. Her husband had been her foundation, her rock. Things were different now. Mosa wrote to him, asking him to stay in Columbia. If she needed help, she would let him know.

Her body healed, but her mind remained an open wound. The days were bearable. There was plenty to keep her occupied. The nights when her eyes couldn't see but her memories were vivid, were a challenge to get through. She waited for the ache in her heart to diminish. Weeks passed. Like a parasite, her grief had taken up residence inside her and refused to leave. Though the experience was a scar that couldn't be seen like those on her back or the one on her face, this new scar hurt much more than the others ever had.

The army had been lying in wait for Gillingham and the four others when they appeared just as Lowenna had said they would. Caught red-handed, even the white jurors couldn't ignore the evidence and together with the black jurors, which the new State Constitution permitted, found them guilty and the defendants were jailed.

Joshua didn't go seeking Lowenna, nor she him. She crossed the street when she saw him after the trial. Her husband might be in prison, but there were plenty of others of the same persuasion. Others who could watch her while her husband was behind bars.

Gillingham was baffled by how the authorities could have got word of the plot. Someone somewhere had betrayed them. That person needed to be found before they could do the same again. Needed to be punished. Needed to be eliminated. Only one thing was worse than the Yankees occupying their homeland, or the niggers who were so full of themselves these days. A Southern traitor.

"It has to be someone I know. Someone I trusted. I just can't think who, but I'll find out if it's the last thing I ever do," he said when his wife visited him in prison before the trial.

Lowenna didn't comment. The slightest hesitancy or nervousness in her voice could start him thinking. Thankfully he didn't know her true past, that she had been married to a Union captain. A captain who had battled his way through South Carolina, laying waste the land in revenge for treason. Gillingham believed she'd married a Virginian who died fighting for the Confederacy, that she had come South in search of the man's aunt where she would have a place to live. She'd claimed she thought the woman lived in Columbia, but clearly she must have been mistaken.

Her husband got five years. Lowenna knew it was wrong to wish someone dead, but she couldn't help but hope, hope that he'd never live long enough to get out.

Eventually, it appeared that the terror which had descended over the South like a shroud might be at an end. A Federal Grand Jury named the KKK a terrorist organization. President Ulysses Grant took a tough line. Hundreds were arrested and martial law declared. It would take time, but by 1872 the Klan had been broken. It would be many years until they rose again. Even the Democrats, hoping to persuade black voters that they could be trusted, began to denounce them.

Maisie went to visit her son.

"Mama, what a pleasant surprise."

"Don't you Mama me," she said as she pushed her way in and began hitting him about the head. "You're a good for nothing, worthless. Worthless..."

Words failed her. Exhausted from her exertions, she sat herself down on a chair in the hallway.

"Why did you do it, Joshua? Why? Your wife is the sweetest, kindest person I know."

"I don't know. I was dumb."

"You sure was. You've dun thrown away the best thing you ever had."

"Can you help me get her back?"

"I don't think so and why should I? You might put her through a whole lot of pain again. She's like a daughter to me, the daughter I never had. I love you son, but I don't like you, not right now at any rate. Being a Representative has made you forget yourself, forget where you come from. You may have fancy clothes and this fancy home, but you've lost your soul. Sold it to the devil himself."

"Please help me. She won't even answer my letters."

"I don't suppose she wants to. Listen, I got Thomas outside. We plan on staying a few days. Mosa don't want him to grow up not knowing his father, but you better be on your best behavior from now on, or you won't be seeing no more of him either."

CHAPTER 14

Mosa took precautions with the following year's cotton crop. She had two men guard it each night, armed with rifles. The yield was average and the price that they got for it not great, but it enabled loan installments to be paid. There was also some profit to share with the others who lived on the plantation. The first money which they had ever been paid in their lives. They received the dollar bills with veneration as though Mosa was giving them pages from the Bible. At last, they would be able to buy something they wanted.

Fall was in the air. Drops of moisture clung like transparent pearls to the grass each morning and there was a welcome coolness to the air after the debilitating torpor of summer's heat.

Mosa came back from inspecting the plantation one afternoon to find Maisie sitting on the step of her hut shivering, even though there were beads of perspiration on her forehead. Mosa placed her hand there.

"You've got a temperature. You need to go to bed and stay there until you get better."

"I'll be fine. Don't you worry about me."

She got up to go but stumbled. Mosa took her by the arm.

"You're not fine. You need to rest. Come along."

She led her to her bed, promising to return with some food when she'd fed Thomas. When she went to visit Maisie later, her condition had deteriorated. She was mumbling incoherently and tossing her head from side to side. Mosa sent one of the men to fetch Joshua. She spent the night applying wet cloths to her forehead, trying to keep her cool.

Joshua arrived with the dawn. Maisie recovered consciousness briefly and smiled.

"You came."

"Of course, Mama. Just rest now. You're gonna be all right." But he and Mosa both knew that probably would not be the case.

He sat one side of the bed, Mosa the other, each holding one of Maisie's hands. As rays from the morning sun penetrated the gaps in the log walls throwing beams of light across the room, Maisie spoke one last time, though she didn't open her eyes.

"I'm coming Nathaniel. Coming to be with you and Jacob."

Salty tears ran down Joshua's face and he hung his head. Mosa came over and placed her hands on his shoulders as she stood behind him.

"I'm so sorry, Joshua. She was the most wonderful woman I ever met."

DAVID CANFORD

Mosa too was bereft. Maisie had been the near-
est thing that she had ever had to a mother. She
owed her very existence to the woman. Maisie had
risked being sold away from her own family to
save Mosa's life.
The funeral was held the same day. After the other
mourners left the graveside, Joshua and Mosa remained, remembering the woman they had loved.
Joshua broke the silence.
"Mosa, you know how sorry I am about what happened. Can't we put it all behind us."
"I don't know that we can. We're different people
to the ones who got married. You've become a successful politician-"
"You wanted me to."
"I did. And what you've achieved is wonderful.
But it just ain't right for us. Our lives are separate
now."
"Come live with me in Columbia. There's plenty
others here. I'm sure Jobe could oversee things."
"No, I belong here. I'd be no good as a society wife
in town."
"Then I'll resign and come back to the plantation."
"No, don't do that. You wouldn't be happy here
now after the life you've gotten used to. Look,
here comes Thomas. He wants to play with you.
Have a safe journey home."
Mosa gave him a weak smile and walked away.
Eventually, Joshua gave up on trying to win Mosa
back. It seemed a hopeless task. Thomas still
visited regularly. Often Mosa would bring him. On

one occasion, a woman was leaving the house as they arrived. She glanced at them in a way that said she knew who they were.

Mosa accepted it. She had offered no compromise. Her days she spent managing the plantation and teaching the young ones. It kept her occupied, too busy to dwell on what might have been.

The sense of loss for her daughter lessened a little, though some days the hurt would return with a crushing intensity as if someone were squeezing her heart in a vice. A baby's cry, or watching little girls running about in the dust, so many things could remind her. She tried to imagine what Martha would have looked like now, tried to imagine the hugs, the kisses, and the laughter. All those priceless moments that she would never experience with her daughter.

Slowly but surely the debt to the bank was decreasing. One more year should just about do it. That would be a huge weight off Mosa's shoulders. She doubted Joshua worried that much about it. The smell of alcohol on his breath when she collected Thomas told her that he had ways of forgetting his worries.

The crop was a good one. Mosa watched it leave on the start of its journey to the coast. On the plantation that evening they held a party. Elijah played his fiddle, and there was dancing and singing almost until the sun came up.

Everyone discussed what they would do with their share of the profit. A new dress and some new clothes for the children, said the mothers. The men talked of replenishing their supplies of tobacco and bourbon. And of course something for their wives, they quickly added to soften their spouses' looks of disapproval.

Mosa began to contemplate getting a new house built to replace the old mansion burned to the ground during the war. Perhaps Joshua was right, borrowing from the bank wasn't such a bad thing. She didn't need a grand place. Three bedrooms would be more than adequate, the usual rooms downstairs and a room which she could use to teach the children. Or maybe even a proper schoolhouse. Yes, she would scale back the size of the house to leave enough to pay for a schoolhouse.

She could offer children on nearby farms the chance of an education too. The public school which had been established was too long a walk for many. Especially those whose parents didn't want them gone most of the day when they were needed to help out and ensure that they produced enough to have sufficient left over for their families once the landowners had taken their cut.

Mosa was happier than she'd felt in a long time. She had a new sense of purpose. Tomorrow would be better. For once, she fell asleep not thinking of that tiny baby who she had only got to hold for so short a time but of how the schoolhouse would look. No more sitting on the hard earth for the kids. A desk for each of them. A big blackboard at the front. Shelves stacked with books. And a large globe so that the children could envision just how big a world they lived in, a wonderful place spoiled only by men's greed and aggression.

When the letter arrived, a crowd gathered around her eager to hear the news. Most of the adults already had a rough idea of how much should have been made.

Mosa smiled at them and opened the envelope. Her smile didn't last. It was replaced by a frown.

"There's some mistake. This ain't right. Don't worry, I'll go see the man I deal with and sort it out."

She didn't bother knocking when she got to his office in town.

"What's the meaning of this?" she demanded putting his letter down on the desk. "It's less than half what we got last year."

"That it is."

"What's going on? Are you trying to increase your take without asking me? We never agreed on an increase."

"No ma'am, I most certainly have not increased my cut. The price of cotton has fallen drastically."

"Why?"

"The depression."

"The what?"

"You folk out in the country sure don't get much news, do you. The whole economy's in a bad way. It's affecting everything. I'm sorry, but pretty much everybody's suffering. I'm probably looking at bankruptcy myself. At least you have your land."

Mosa had already done the math in her head. They would default on their loan before next year's crop was sold. She must go see Joshua. The bank needed to be spoken to and asked to be patient.

When she arrived at his house, Joshua was snoring in an armchair as dribble ran from his mouth and down his chin. An almost empty bottle of bourbon stood on the table next to him.

"Joshua, wake up."

"Ugh?"

"The price of cotton's halved. We don't have enough to satisfy the bank. You need to go talk to them."

His pupils disappeared as his eyelids closed and his head rolled forward onto his chest. Mosa gave up trying to wake him and proceeded to the bank herself.

"Let me get your records," said the clerk after she had explained the situation.

Nervous about the outcome, she tapped her fingers on the arms of the chair as she waited. He didn't return with any papers.

"The bank sold your loan. We received a good offer for it. We're offloading a lot of loans in the current challenging economic climate."

"Who to?"

"I didn't check. Anyway if you haven't received our letter, you soon will. You'll need to negotiate with whoever bought the loan. I can't help you any further. Good day."

Mosa returned to Joshua's. He was still sleeping. She looked around the room. On the dresser she found an unopened letter. Two unopened letters, one hidden behind the other. Both were addressed to them.

The first was the promised letter from the bank. It informed them who the loan and the mortgage over their land had been assigned to. The second letter contained even more unwelcome news.

CHAPTER 15

Once again Mosa was back at the place which she'd hoped she would never have to revisit and once more he was sitting on his veranda. It was almost as if he had been waiting there ever since his letter had been mailed, not wishing to miss the sight of her arrival so that he could savor every moment of his triumph.

"Good day to you, Mosa. Won't you come join me up here and sit down. What can I offer you to drink?"

"Nothing, thank you." She ignored his offer to sit.

"How can I help you?"

Gregory Brown had a mischievous look in his eye. Of course he knew exactly why she had come.

"You bought our loan off the bank."

"Yes, it seemed like a good investment. Did I make a mistake? Can't you pay?"

"In time we can. I expect you already know the cotton price has halved this year."

"I do indeed."

"Then why have you sent us a letter demanding full repayment immediately?"

"To protect myself. Who knows how bad the situation may have gotten in a year's time?"

"But we can't pay you now."

"In that case you give me no choice but to enforce my rights. The lawyers will handle it. The land is being auctioned to the highest bidder. Tomorrow."

"Tomorrow?"

"Yes. Seems to me, Mosa, that you've been very careless. How often have I offered to buy your land at a good price. Always you refused."

"Please. Think of all those families who will suffer."

"They'll be just fine. The new owner will want laborers."

"Is there nothing I can do to persuade you to give us time?"

"Well..." He stroked the end of his nose with his index finger. "It's lonely here since my wife passed and you're a fine looking woman, Mosa, even if you ain't white."

Mosa's face filled with anger faster than a chameleon changing color.

"You have absolutely no shame, do you. I'd rather starve. And when I think of all those poor slave girls you raped, it makes me so mad. You're a wicked man Gregory Brown."

Brown leaped to his feet.

"Get the hell off my property right now!"

When Mosa spoke, her tone was as smooth and cool as ice.

"Gladly. But just remember, you may have got away with a lot on this earth, but we all face the Lord's judgment in the end. There's no hiding from that. Not even for you."

The high from the adrenaline pumping through her body from finally getting to call out that odious man for what he was, faded rapidly as reality sunk in. The land was lost. Her dreams of a schoolhouse vanished into thin air. And those living there now would face a much harsher future when they found themselves virtual slaves again. Tied to the property to toil endlessly, without ever being able to accumulate sufficient money to allow them or their children to break away and find something that would give them a decent living.

"Did you sort out the mistake?" asked one of the men when she returned.

All had gathered to hear her news upon seeing her coming down the track.

"It was no mistake. The price of cotton has collapsed."

"Well, we hunker down and carry on. Next year, it'll be better."

"There won't be no next year. The bank sold the loan to Gregory Brown. He's demanded immediate repayment which he knows we can't make, just so he can sell Old Oaks. I'm so very sorry. I'm sure you'll all be offered work. It just won't be as good as it was before."

"Don't you worry about us, Mosa. You gave us a

real chance to make something of ourselves," said one of the women. "Nobody's ever done that before. But what about you? Have you decided what you'll do?"

"Not yet," said Mosa, fooling herself that she had options.

She waited until they got word of who the new owner would be. Her suspicions about the integrity of the auction were confirmed. Gregory Brown bought it for only fifty dollars. The word was no one else turned up. Mosa doubted anyone had even been told about it.

She left with Thomas on the cart in the dead of night, skulking away like a fox. Mosa didn't feel she had the strength to say goodbye without breaking down. Instead, she left a note thanking them all for their friendship and kindness, apologizing once again that it hadn't worked out, and wishing them well for the future.

As they rode, tears ran down her face like raindrops on a window pane. All her dreams had turned to dust. All that effort. All that worry. All for nothing.

Yet she still had her son. He was her sun and her moon, more precious than anything else. She would pick herself up again for him. In her life she had faced worse and come through it, and she would this time. Somehow.

It was early morning when they reached Columbia. Thomas was still sleeping, his head on her lap. She waited, not wanting to intrude on any overnight guest. Sure enough, the lady she had seen before departed as the town awoke.

"Hello, Joshua," said Mosa as he emerged a short while later.

"I wasn't expecting to see you again so soon. You brought Thomas?"

"Yeah, he's still asleep. Can I come in? I'd rather not give you the news in public."

"What news?" he asked as she stepped down from the cart and walked inside.

"We lost the plantation. The bank sold the loan to Gregory Brown and he foreclosed. He had a phoney auction and sold it to himself for next to nothing."

"How come I didn't know? The bank's supposed to write to us here."

"They did. You were asleep drunk when I found the letters here. They were unopened."

"Oh, right. I've been so busy. I hadn't had a chance-"

"It's OK, Joshua. I'm not here to pass judgment on you. I was hoping maybe Thomas and I could stay here a short while until I find some work. I won't get in your way. There's no need to stop your friend visiting."

"How do you-"

"I saw her leaving. So can we stay?"

"Of course, as long as you like. She won't be coming no more. It'll be good to be a family again."

"Please don't stop her coming on my account."

"Let me get your bag and carry the boy in."

CHAPTER 16

Mosa's plans to find a job were thwarted by the bad economic situation. So many were out of work and there were no vacancies.

Much as she hadn't wanted to, Mosa was obliged to rely on Joshua. Not that he made her unwelcome. On the contrary, he made a great effort to be agreeable. The woman who Mosa had seen never returned, and the bottles of alcohol disappeared from view.

She ate her meals with Thomas, and on the evenings when Joshua didn't have an engagement, she cooked for him. One evening, she accepted his invitation to stay and talk while he ate.

"I know I've said it before but I do so regret my one night fling with Lowenna. I was such an idiot."

"Well, she is a ravishing beauty, and I guess no man is gonna turn it down if it's offered to him on a plate."

"She didn't. It was my fault. I made the move when she came round here."

"Then why did she come round? Any woman knows you don't go visiting a man alone, especially at night unless you have an ulterior motive."

"We'd met by chance in the street one day. I asked her to meet for a coffee. I wanted to get her news and tell you, but that didn't go as planned. She's married a diehard Confederate, not out of affection it would seem, but to find some security for her son. That night you found us, she'd come here to warn me that she'd overheard her husband and others plotting to attack a Republican picnic, a gathering I was to have been at. I alerted the authorities and they were there waiting for them. They threw them in jail."

Mosa said nothing for a while, processing the news.

"It sounds like she saved your life then."

"Most certainly, yes. When they were caught, they were fully armed and clearly intent on killing as many of us as they could. Mosa, do you think you'll ever be able to forgive me for what I did?"

"I already have. I used to think not doing so would somehow help me cope. It didn't. It only made things worse."

"Do you think we could try again then?"

"I really don't know. I need to get on with clearing up. I'll see you in the morning."

In the first store Mosa inquired at the following day, she got her answer. She went to the address they had given her. The door was opened by a maid who asked her to wait though she didn't invite her in, shutting the door in her face and leaving her standing outside.

"Follow me," she said as she reopened the door and directed her into the parlor.

Lowenna stood there, rubbing her hands together anxiously. Like a child about to be admonished, her eyes rested only briefly on Mosa before seeking refuge by looking away to one side.

"Hello, Lowenna."

"I'm so ashamed, Mosa. I very much regret-"

"I'm not after an apology. I'm here to thank you, thank you for saving Joshua's life. My son would have been without a father if not for you."

Lowenna dropped her hands to her sides. The tension which had been eating at her was gone. She looked Mosa in the face.

"That is very kind of you."

"Not really. You were brave to do what you did."

"Maybe, but then so stupid. I'd offer you refreshment, but my husband doesn't take kindly to..."

"To colored folk?"

"Yes."

"I understand. I only wanted to let you know how I felt."

"I'm so grateful that you did. I have felt truly awful about what I did to you for so long."

"Well, goodbye Lowenna. I hope we part as friends."

"Indeed, we do."

As she made her way back across town, Mosa's route was blocked by a parade. Though it was no Fourth of July parade. Armed men on horses wearing red shirts passed by to cheers from the white people watching them. Most white women in town had taken to putting red ribbons in their hair to show their support. Those who saw Mosa gave her a look that needed no words to interpret and she disappeared into the first alleyway that she reached.

Joshua had told her of the "Red Shirts". The Klan may have been defeated for now but a new white supremacist group had arisen in South Carolina. With black registered voters outnumbering whites, the white population wasn't accepting of democracy. It would never give them back control.

As the Federal Government tired of having to spend money to protect African Americans from whites in the South, the Red Shirts sensed their time had come. Their agenda was to win the forthcoming election by murder, intimidation, and rigging the ballot box.

Lowenna's wish that her husband shouldn't survive his incarceration hadn't been granted. Thackery Gillingham had been released some months ago. Jail hadn't reformed him, only embittered him more. Being guarded by black prison warders had become for him yet another grievance to add to the many which he already harbored. To him, the Civil War had been a war of Northern aggression, Yankees imposing their will on the South and extinguishing its freedom to determine how it should live. A view so many whites in the South subscribed to and would continue to cling to, considering themselves to be the victims.

"Who would have believed a few years ago that niggers would have been in a position of power? And negro soldiers patrolling our streets. Our Republic is rotten to the core. I'm only glad my parents never lived to see this day."

Lowenna passed no comment as they sat eating lunch.

"Cat got your tongue, woman?"

"No, but on political matters I defer to your judgment."

"That don't mean you can't voice your support. Sometimes I wonder about you."

And he did. He no longer trusted anyone, not even his wife. His friends assured him that they'd kept an eye on her and hadn't noticed anything untoward, but he didn't believe that a young woman like her would have lived like a nun for these past five years.

"There's a rally for the Democrats tomorrow evening. I expect you to accompany me. And be sure to wear red ribbons in your hair."

CHAPTER 17

"This election is gonna be the toughest we've ever faced," said Joshua as he and Mosa sat in the kitchen chatting that evening.

"All the more reason you should let me help."

"It could be dangerous."

"Being colored is dangerous, Joshua. We live with that danger every single day of our lives."

"Yes, you're right. There's a Republican rally tomorrow evening. You could come along and talk with the other wives. See how you can get involved."

"I will."

"Thank you. It's been tough at times without your support. I only did it to make you proud of me. And maybe I did until I messed up. You were the love of my life, Mosa, and you always will be."

Mosa reached out across the table and touched his hand for a brief moment. Maybe he wasn't so different from the man who she had married.

"I'm going to bed now, Joshua. Goodnight."

Joshua stayed up for a while working on his speech for the rally before retiring. When he went upstairs, his heart skipped a beat to see his bedroom bathed in the soft light of candles and Mosa lying in his bed. She smiled.

"I'm ready to try again."

The following evening, they walked hand in hand to the venue. A sizeable crowd had already gathered at the hall. Joshua went to the front and called for attention.

"Thank Y'all for coming. Your vote this fall is more important than ever. The Democrats-"

"Yeah, well maybe it's about time they had a chance. We got the vote, but we ain't got no money and no jobs," shouted out one angry man. Others joined in the heckling.

Across town, Thackery Gillingham was at the Democrat rally, cheering on Wade Hampton, a former Confederate Officer and their candidate for Governor. He looked an almost biblical figure with his large bushy beard and thick mustache. To his supporters he was indeed a savior, a man who could at last wrest control of the State from the Republicans. Red Shirts stood proudly behind the man, rifles slung over their shoulders as he ranted maniacally.

"The people's money is being stolen. Our Legislature is made up of a majority of negroes, most of whom can neither read nor write. They are as dirty a band of robbers as ever disgraced State government. There are wild orgies going on in the State House about every night. This is white man's country and white men must govern it. We have been pushed around long enough."

His speech was received with loud cheering.

Lowenna had pleaded a migraine. Initially chagrined by her non-attendance, Gillingham was now in a better mood, uplifted by the atmosphere of hate and bigotry.

Fired up by the rhetoric, some of the Red Shirts departed. Gillingham stayed chatting. Even months after his release, people still wanted to shake him by the hand. To those who thought like him, he was a hero. He relished the adulation.

"Sir, I'm honored to make your acquaintance," said a man of similar age to himself. "I heard what you did and how a rigged jury of niggers convicted you. If Hampton gets elected, we can bring an end to rule by monkeys."

"I couldn't agree more. And you are, sir?"

"Gregory Brown, at your service. I own a couple of plantations west of here. I hear you too lost your sons in the war as did I."

"Unfortunately, yes. They gave their lives for us, which is why we must carry on the fight otherwise they will have died in vain."

"I couldn't agree more. My wife never recovered from the loss. The grief eventually killed her."

"Yes, a terrible thing. I lost my wife too. Still, I found me a new one."

"Is she here tonight?"

"No, Lowenna is indisposed."

"Lowenna? Now that's an unusual name, and not one I thought I'd ever hear again."

"You intrigue me, sir."

"Dare say it's purely a coincidence, but I once met a lady by that name. Striking red hair she had. She was living on a nigger controlled plantation near me for a while. Can't be the same person though. She'd been married to a Yankee captain, part of Sherman's rabble of outlaws that ransacked our State. Came to live down here with Mosa Elwood, a mulatto who'd inherited the plantation next to mine. Seemed that Lowenna's husband died there, protecting the niggers."

"Can you excuse me. There's someone I need to talk to."

He didn't, but Gillingham needed to absorb this information alone. As he marched home, Brown's words resounded inside his head like cannonballs exploding. Gillingham fought to control his emotions. A rage such as he had never felt had taken over his entire being.

It all made perfect sense now. Her reticence. The doubts that he'd carried about where she really came from. And only yesterday his maid, who he'd asked to tell him of any visitors, had informed him that a Mosa Elwood had called to see her. What business could she possibly have had with his wife unless they already knew each other? And now he knew exactly how the two women had become acquainted.

His own wife was the snake. The one who must have betrayed him and his men, the one who had been responsible for them spending years in jail.

He'd kill her with his bare hands if he had to.

Reaching the house, he thundered up the stairs. He flung open the door to Lowenna's bedroom. She was seated in a chair embroidering.

"I thought you had a migraine."

"Oh, it went away. Is everything all right, you look a little flustered?"

"Flustered ain't the beginning of it."

He struck her hard across the face with the back of his hand.

"Ow! What did you do that for?"

"I know who you are now. An imposter. A traitor."

He hit her again, causing her to fall off the chair and onto the floor.

"Get up."

She backed toward the wall, her eyes reflecting her terror. His look was wild, his breathing like that of a bison preparing to charge.

"Married to a Yankee captain, eh?"

"I don't know what-"

"Stop lying to me or your son ain't gonna see the morning."

CHAPTER 18

"Oh no, please don't hurt him," pleaded Lowenna.

"Well, start telling the truth."

"OK, OK. I will."

Her words were breathless, uttered in desperation.

"You were the one that warned the army that night, weren't you?"

"I...I overheard what you were planning. I went to warn Joshua Elwood. I didn't want him to die. He and his wife had been so kind to me. They took me in after my first husband was killed and we had nowhere to live."

Gillingham considered what to do. The boy was asleep. A gunshot would wake him as well as the cook and the maid.

"You'll stay in this room and not make a sound."

"What about Abe?"

"If you do as I say, he'll go off to school as usual in the morning, and then I'll deal with you."

"But you won't hurt him. Promise me."

"If you don't try anything, he'll be left unharmed. I'll send him to an orphanage. If they won't take him in, he can live on the streets. I'm not keeping a child of yours under my roof."

He took the key from her door and locked it from the outside. He would kill her after the boy was out of the house and dispose of the body. Others mustn't know what she'd done. He would look such a fool for having married her. The shame of it would be a humiliation he couldn't bear.

The boy too. He'd have to be dealt with. Gillingham would say that they had gone to visit family in England. In due course, he could inform friends they'd been taken by the fever whilst there.

At the Republican gathering, Joshua was continuing to have a hard time. He didn't put it past the Democrats to have planted the hecklers. Mosa was taken aback by the vitriol displayed. It wasn't at all how she imagined a rally would be. Joshua's life was far from as easy as she had thought.

Suddenly, the doors at the back of the hall burst open. In marched Red Shirts, their boots echoing off the wooden floor like rapid gunfire. Reaching the front, they turned and faced the audience. They stood in a straight line, a few paces apart as if a firing squad. The crowd didn't know whether to throw themselves on the floor for protection, or try and make a run for it. Undecided, they were cowed. One of the Red Shirts climbed up onto the stage.

"Don't listen to this man. The Republicans are nothing but a bunch of crooks. Stealing your taxes to enrich themselves."

"Get out of our meeting."

In his anger, Joshua pushed the man away.

"Don't you dare lay a finger on me. You filthy nigger."

The man moved back a little. Raising his rifle, he fired at point blank range. Joshua's legs buckled and he collapsed onto the floor. Stunned silence gripped the crowd.

"Let that be a warning to the rest of you. Turn up to vote and you'll meet the same fate."

Mosa rushed forward, pushing past all to get to the stage and comfort Joshua. Getting down on her knees beside him, she placed her hands on his chest in a fruitless attempt to stem the flow of blood.

For a moment she glanced upward, her face locking with that of the man who had shot her husband. His expression was one of utter contempt. He jerked his head at his companions and they left as quickly as they had arrived.

"Joshua. Joshua."

He didn't hear her, it was already too late. Mosa cradled his head, the blood from her hands smeared on his face. Numbness enveloped her like a thick fog.

"Come dear. The men will sort this out. Let's get you home."

It was a white woman. One of the Republican wives who she had been chatting to earlier. She reached out her hand to Mosa.

"Home? Yes, home. I must get home."

"I'll come with you."

"There's no need."

"But-"

"No need."

"I'll drop by in the morning then to see what we can do to help."

Mosa didn't reply, she was already heading for the door. She hurried home as fast as her legs would let her. Panic had seized her. What if?

Opening his door, a surge of relief swept through her to see Thomas safe and sound and fast asleep.

In her room, she lay on her bed curled up in a fetal position as she wept. When she could cry no more, she lay there thinking, thinking and remembering. Every man that she had ever loved had been killed. Thomas, Lloyd, and now Joshua.

She couldn't let the same happen to her son. Mosa hadn't wanted her life to be defined by fear, but she had a child to think about. He would never be safe in this place. They needed to get away from here, get out of South Carolina. Freedom hadn't brought safety from the white man's violence. Maybe it never would. They didn't see black people any differently to what they always had. What, if anything, would change their attitude? Nothing was ever going to change in this State.

Mosa slept little. Come morning, she cuddled Thomas as he cried at the news she had to give him.

While he half-heartedly ate some breakfast, she packed a bag. They wouldn't wait until after the funeral. She couldn't face burying yet another person who she had loved. And what if the Red Shirts intended to silence her so that she couldn't identify her husband's killer? That man had seen who she was and knew that she had seen him. He probably knew where they lived or would soon find out. It was too dangerous to stay a moment longer. Lowenna too had barely slept. She didn't trust her husband's word. Killing her son would mean nothing to him. Not now Gillingham knew what she had done and who she really was. But there was nothing she could do. She was locked in her second floor room with no means of escape.

Gillingham's voice was sharp like thorns.

"Time to get up boy and off to school."

"Where's mom?"

"She's in bed with a headache. You'll see her tonight. Hurry or you'll be late."

Lowenna hung her head in her hands. She wanted to shout out. Shout out to Abraham. Tell him to run, run and not come back. But Thackery might catch him before he could get away. She imagined her son's screams for help, the agony of not being able to protect him.

There must be something which she could do. Something.

She looked at the window. Inch by inch she pushed the brass bed toward it, her heart in her mouth each time the wooden floorboards creaked. Pulling the sheets off the bed, she tied them together and the end of one to the bed frame.

She waited. She recognized the sound of Thomas noisily descending the staircase two by two and the way he slammed the front door as he left the house. Gillingham wasted no time once Abraham had gone to school.

"Dolly, come here."

"Yes, sir?"

"You can take the day off. Go see your family."

"Sir?"

"I'm feeling generous. Quick, get out of here before I change my mind. Tell cook too. I don't need either of you back until tomorrow morning."

"Why thank you, sir."

Lowenna heard the two women leave. They were in high spirits. She threw the sheets out. They nearly reached the ground.

His footsteps were heavy and resolute as he came up the stairs. Lowenna climbed out and began to descend. Before she was halfway down, there was a ripping sound. She fell holding a sheet that was no longer attached. Fortunately, she fell on a flower bed. She was unhurt.

Getting quickly to her feet, Lowenna picked up her dress to avoid tripping over it and ran across the lawn. She looked back only once. Her husband was at her window, aiming his pistol.

CHAPTER 19

Lowenna heard it. She would feel its bite and then darkness would fall like a guillotine.

But it didn't.

Energized by her narrow escape, Lowenna ran like she never had before. Ran until she could no more and had to succumb to brisk walking. Then up ahead, she saw him.

"Abe."

"Mom?"

She grabbed the gangly fourteen year old by the hand. He threw it off.

"What's going on?"

"I'll tell you later. Just do what I ask and you'll be all right."

Frequently glancing behind her, Lowenna steered the boy toward the station. Smoke was rising above the building. She didn't stop to buy a ticket. There might not be time. A whistle blew just as she pushed her son onto the train.

Looking out from the door as they departed, Lowenna saw Gillingham arrive on the platform astride his horse. But he couldn't catch her. Not anymore. Yet his look wasn't what she would have expected.

"Where are we going?" protested her son.

"Away from here. Your stepfather's a bad man."

"What's he done?"

"I can't tell you here. Come let's find a seat."

The car they had boarded was crowded. They made their way through to another, in the far half of which only two were seated. A woman and a boy. The seats opposite them empty as were those around them. The other travelers, who were white, had chosen to sit crammed together rather than near them.

Lowenna went to go sit there.

"Mom, stop. We can't go sit with niggers."

"Be quiet, Abe."

The woman looked up as they sat down.

"Lowenna."

"Mosa."

"Is this your son? My how you've grown."

Abraham looked out of the window, disgruntled that his mother was making them sit with such people.

"And Thomas too is growing up fast. Are you traveling to Charleston?"

"Yes, and then we're leaving South Carolina. The Red Shirts shot Joshua. We're not safe here."

"Oh no. I'm so dreadfully sorry. I can't believe it. That's terrible."

Thomas kept his head down the entire time as he held his mother's hand. Abraham ignored them all, still staring out of the window and sulking.

He knew about the Red Shirts. He had cheered their parade with his classmates. His teacher told them they were fighting for the white man's freedom. That Joshua must have done something to deserve it. Niggers were a threat. They'd kill every white man, woman, and child if they got a chance. Every right thinking white person knew that. He should never have come with his mother. She was only a woman. How could she understand what was at stake.

"We're leaving too. Thackeray found out about me. He was going to kill me."

That grabbed Abraham's attention.

"Mom, what are you talking about? You gotta tell me."

"Your father, Lloyd Jenkins, wasn't a Confederate soldier like I told you. He was a captain in the Union Army. He died fighting in this State to save people. People such as Mosa here. After he died, we had no money. Mosa let us come live on her plantation. You were too little probably to remember."

Abraham did have memories, confused and incomplete like a half remembered dream. A small shadowy hut, unfamiliar faces, clinging tightly to his mother as they rode off on a horse at night. They didn't create a whole, but they still had the capacity to frighten him when he lay in bed at night so he'd pushed them to the farthest recesses of his mind.

"Some years back, I found out that your stepfather was going to lead an attack on a Republican meeting and kill people so I warned them."

"What? You mean you betrayed him, and now you're telling me my father wasn't fighting for the Confederacy but a goddamn Yankee. You're a liar. I hate you. I'm getting off at the next stop. I'm going back home. I'm not gonna sit with you, or no niggers."

He tried to get up from his seat and past his mother.

"Stop. Sit right down this minute and show some respect. I know this must all be a big shock to you. But you can't go back. I made Thackery promise me he wouldn't harm you. He said he wouldn't have you living under his roof. Would send you to the orphanage. I don't believe him. If you go back, he'll most probably kill you."

"You've ruined my life. I was happy in Columbia. I had friends. It was home. You've lied to me, to him. To everyone. How could you do this?"

"Your Mama's a good person," said Mosa. "Everything she did, she did to protect you. To give you the best life she could."

"What business is it of yours?"

"Abe-"

"It's OK, Lowenna. I knew your father. Knew him when I was in New York. He was a fine and noble man. He believed in freedom and equality for all. That the Declaration of Independence should apply to everyone. I was there when he died. The last thing he ever said, the last thing he ever asked for, was that I should let your mom and you know just how much he loved you both.

"I know how hard it is when you first find out where you actually came from, and find out who you really are. It may not feel like it right now, but one day you'll be glad. Glad about who you are."

Abraham said nothing. He turned and looked out of the window once more. His world had just drowned.

"Thank you," mouthed Lowenna.

The four of them sat in contemplation, each lost in thought of how the last twenty-four hours had completely upended their lives. The stability which they thought they had, gone. Gone without a warning. Rocked by the rhythm of the train's motion, both boys eventually fell asleep.

"Where will you go, Mosa?"

"Up North, I guess. Though having lived there, I know it's not that much better than here for the likes of Thomas and I. How about you?"

"I plan to return to England."

"England? Won't they throw you in jail, or ship you off to Australia?"

"Unlikely. I don't intend going back to Cornwall, and I doubt in the rest of the country anyone would be looking for me any longer even if they ever were. Why don't you come with us? You wouldn't be all alone then."

"But it's thousands of miles away."

"Yes, thousands of miles away from all of this.

DAVID CANFORD

You'd be safe there."
"I don't think so. It's too far."
Mosa reminisced how Thomas, her brother, had dreamed of going to Europe one day. A dream which he had never been able to fulfill.
Lowenna watched the telegraph poles pass by. Sending messages faster than a man could ride, faster than a train could travel.
A feeling grew inside her, as though her stomach had become a knot with someone pulling it ever tighter. Thackery knew where she was going. He couldn't catch her, but a telegram would be there before she was. That look on his face at the station, it hadn't been one of anger or frustration, not a look of defeat. It had been more a smirk, a look of self-satisfaction.

CHAPTER 20

The train was slowing down now. Countryside gave way to buildings. They were close to their destination. No time to delay.

"We're getting off. I'm worried Thackery will have people waiting for us at the station. He saw us get on. He could have sent a telegram. Take good care of yourself, Mosa. Wake up, Abe."

"What now?"

"We're getting off here. Quick, move yourself."

She pushed him toward the door.

"Wait, we're coming with you."

Mosa pulled Thomas by the hand. When they caught up outside the car on the metal platform, Abraham was protesting.

"This isn't the station. The train's still moving."

It was, though not much faster than a person could walk.

"You need to get off here if you don't want Thackery's men to get you. He saw us get on the train. He will have sent a telegram and have his contacts waiting for us, I'm convinced of it."

Abraham didn't know what was true any longer.

But it sounded plausible. He climbed onto the bottom step and hopped off. The others followed. For a moment, they all watched the train rumble on down the track.

"Why are they here with us?" demanded Abraham.

"Because they're our friends. You've been brought up in a world where people have told you a lot of things which aren't right. They've taught you that you should hate and despise certain people. That's not your fault. In time, you'll come to understand that those who told you such things were wrong."

"Hmm," her son grunted. "What are we going to do now?"

"You like adventure stories, don't you?"

"Yes."

"Well, now you're going on a real adventure. We're going to England."

"Oh no I'm not."

"Stay here then and live on the streets if that's what you want. We're off with or without you. Come on, Mosa and Thomas."

Lowenna's gamble worked. They'd only gone a few steps when he began following, even if he did keep his distance and give his mother a surly teenage stare each time she turned to check that he was still behind them.

Retreating from the railroad, they made their way along the sidewalks to the port, guided by ships' masts rising above the buildings. All the while the two mothers looked about them. They were tense. The train would have reached the station by now. Any men waiting for Lowenna and her son could be prowling the streets, searching for them. Once at the harbor, Lowenna went off to ask about sailings.

"There's a boat going out later today bound for Bristol. They're willing to accommodate us, so I booked our passage."

"How much-"

"No need to worry about that. I've been stashing cash away for a long time." Lowenna leaned forward and whispered into Mosa's ear. "I sowed pockets inside this dress. I'm virtually a walking bank."

Mosa couldn't help but laugh.

"While we wait, we better get these two boys fed. Abe's like a bear with a sore head when he's hungry."

As the evening sun descended below the horizon, their ship slipped quietly out to sea. The enormity of what she was doing suddenly hit Mosa. She was seized with doubt. What had possessed her to do this? She had been rash. Her world, everything which she had ever known, was minute by minute getting farther out of reach. This wasn't the same as sailing up the coast to New York as she had done several years ago. However, it was already a decision which couldn't be changed. There was no going back.

Mosa remained on deck until the land had merged with the night, flowing in like an incoming tide above her. Thomas was already deep in the land of dreams when she slipped into bed in their tiny cabin.

He'd had no doubts, effervescent with excitement as they'd climbed aboard. Never had he seen anything so big or tall. Nor had he seen the ocean before. He had endless questions for the English crew about sea monsters and mermaids. They laughed and assured him that they'd seen such. He would just have to keep his eyes open as they rarely appeared above the surface for more than a second or two.

The ship itself was a playground like none that he'd ever experienced. So many ups and downs, places to climb, places to explore, and places to hide. He hoped the journey would take weeks.

Mosa was happy that her son still had the unrestrained enthusiasm of childhood. It would help him overcome their loss. In the days which followed, she rarely saw him other than at meal times.

They didn't see much of Abraham either, and when they did it wasn't a pleasant experience. He was still seething with resentment that his life had been turned upside down, still unhappy that his father wasn't who he thought he had been. It was as though he had his very own dark cloud above him as he moped about the ship.

Mosa and Lowenna were the only two women on board and spent most of their waking hours in each other's company.

"Abe worries me. I thought he'd be coming round a

little by now."

"Give him time. When your identity is different to what you've spent your whole life believing, it's a big deal. Believe me. It certainly was for me."

"You?"

"Yes, my parents were white. There was an African way back in my father's ancestry which showed up in me. I was disowned. I spent years thinking I was the result of my mother having to accept the advances of some white man. I got told she died before I ever knew her. I was older than Abe when I found out the truth. I know I struggled for some time to cope with it. It's probably even harder at his age. But he has a loving mother which I never did. He'll be fine, just you wait and see."

"Yes, I'm sure you're right. Mosa, there's something I wanted to ask you. On the train you said you knew Lloyd in New York. I didn't know that. You've never mentioned it before."

"Yeah, I probably should have told you earlier. I felt awkward about it. I left the South and went to New York once my brother had secured my freedom. I met Lloyd at a Republican rally. We became friends."

"Friends?"

"Well, more than that. We were to marry after he came back from the war. But then he met you. I'm glad he did. By the time we met again when he came to the plantation, I'd already met Joshua."

"Seems then like our destinies were entwined even before we met."

"Yes, I guess it does."

CHAPTER 21

The ocean seemed never ending as if they would sail on into oblivion. Each morning, Mosa emerged on deck expecting to see a change. Apart from the size of the swell and the water alternating between gray and dark blue, it was the same as the day before and the day before that.

When she heard someone shout "Land ahoy" early one evening, she almost tripped in her rush to reach the bow. Though the crew assured her, she could still see nothing but water. The Scilly Isles they told her, an archipelago thirty miles off the English coast, was out there on the horizon.

Come morning, they were passing a wild coast of dark cliffs and crashing waves. Waves which, like them, had come out of the Atlantic Ocean and were now dying in foam and spray as they crashed onto the rocks.

"That's Cornwall, my home," said Lowenna.

"It's beautiful."

"It's a deceptive beauty, one that seduces you even though it'll never nurture you. Most who live there barely get by."

"Not much different to South Carolina by the sound of it."

They docked in Bristol the following morning. To Mosa, it was strange to be in a place where every face that she could see was white. Many stared at her and her son as they walked through the town. It was an experience which she didn't enjoy. At home that had only happened when she visited the bank for the first time.

Sensing her friend's discomfort, Lowenna didn't hold back, directly confronting some.

"What's the matter with you? Have you never seen a lady this beautiful before? Now get out of our way and mind your own business."

The onlookers were too surprised to answer and drew back.

"Some people," muttered Lowenna.

"Well, it's at least good to be on dry land again," said Mosa.

"I hate this country, it's cold," complained Abraham.

Thick clouds hid the sun and a brisk wind blew down the narrow street they were on.

"This is summer, Abe. Enjoy it while it lasts. Anyway, the heat in South Carolina is exhausting. Now, first things first. I need to find somewhere to change my money, and then find us a place to stay."

"Don't go lifting your dress in a bank or they'll throw you out," chuckled Mosa.

"I took it all out last night. It's all here in this bag under the clothes I bought before we left Charleston. Look, there's a bank. Wait here a minute."

Though naturally pale, Mosa had never seen Lowenna look the way she did when she came out of the building. Her skin had a sallow tint to it.

"Are you sick?"

"The money. It's gone. Someone's taken it. It must have happened on the ship."

"Great. Stuck in this horrible place with no money," moaned her son.

"That's not helpful, Abe."

Mosa touched Lowenna's arm.

"I have some, not a lot. But enough to keep us fed and find us a place to stay while we look for work."

Rats scurried across the floorboards at night and the rooms they rented had an unpleasant smell. The walls were decorated with damp.

The two women found work in a factory, making cotton balls from cotton shipped over from the United States. Mosa wondered if any of it had come from what had once been her plantation.

The machines were deafening and the hours long. It was as hard as working in the cotton fields, worse in fact. There she had got to be outside in the fresh air, got to see the sun and feel the rain, and she had been able to talk to those she was working with. In the factory, it was too noisy to hold a conversation.

Mosa was concerned one evening when they arrived back to find no sign of Thomas.

"Hey Abe, have you seen Thomas?"

"Said he was going out, didn't say where."

128

When he hadn't returned come dark, Mosa went out searching for him. At night the city's alleys filled with drunkards and brawls. The atmosphere was ugly. Mosa ignored the shouts for her attention, the demands for a kiss and more. She shook off the hands that tried to grab her. Her fear for her son was greater than any concern for her own safety.

Though she walked miles, she couldn't find him. Frantic with worry, Mosa slapped Thomas across the face when she returned to find him already back.

"Don't you ever do that again. You know I've told you not to go out without telling me."

"I'm sorry."

"You should be. Just where were you? I've been out for hours searching for you."

"I found a job washing dishes. I thought I'd get back before you did, but they made me stay for a long time. Here's the money they gave me."

Mosa regretted her rush to judgment and hugged him close.

Though the two women never complained, each intuitively sensed the other felt the same. They regretted their decision to come, but it was too late now. Returning to America required money they didn't have.

Mosa applied for teaching jobs. She didn't get them. Here racism was sugar-coated. There were expressions of regret, but they couldn't hide true feelings. The pinched smiles, the whispers as she turned her back, and sometimes before she had.

The morning sickness took Mosa by surprise. She wondered how they would cope when she had the baby, even more so when the boss fired her upon discovering that she was pregnant.

Lowenna and Abraham fought constantly, she berating him for not working and helping to bring in money, he blaming her for bringing him to England.

One day as Mosa sat in the bedroom she shared with Thomas, Abraham flung open the door.

"You can tell mom I've got a job like she wanted me to. I'm off to sea. There's nothing for me here."

"You can stay and tell her yourself when she gets back from work."

Her words were spoken to the door. He had already gone.

CHAPTER 22

Lowenna ran down to the docks after work. When she saw her returning up the hill, Mosa could tell from the way her shoulders sagged that she hadn't found him. Mosa held her close as she wept.

After a long and dreary winter, Maisie was born on a bright spring morning. Lowenna was there to deliver her. The two women shed tears of joy. The baby had her daddy's eyes, and at long last Mosa had the little girl she wanted.

Thomas was enchanted with his new sister, and took care of her during the day so that Mosa could work. She found another factory job. It was no more pleasant than her first one but it brought in money.

Even with both mothers earning, there still seemed to be precious little left over once they had paid the landlord and fed the family. Just like back home, the great majority struggled to survive.

On her day off each Sunday, Lowenna would visit the docks, hoping her son's boat might have returned or that at least someone might have news of him. She put on a brave face, although Mosa knew how her heart must be breaking.

"There'll be news next week, I'm sure of it," said Lowenna.

Bristol was a busy city. Its streets clogged with people and too many horses. Accidents were commonplace.

It happened in a split second as Mosa made her way back from work early one evening. A small boy ran out in front of her. He wasn't looking. A horse and cart were only feet away, the driver unaware of the little person directly in his path. Quick as a hawk swooping down on its prey, Mosa snatched him, pulling him out of harm's way. He squirmed and yelled, annoyed that his dash for freedom had been ended.

"Henry, you mustn't run away like that."

A man in top hat and tails arrived.

"Thank you so much, madam. Edward de Montfort at your service." He removed his hat and tipped it forward in greeting. "I'm afraid my son got away from me. I saw what you did. You have saved him from serious injury or worse. How can I repay you?"

"Think nothing of it."

"There must be something surely."

"I wish only for a job to match my skills, but I doubt you could help with that."

"Exactly what is your skill?"

"I'm a teacher."

"Do you have references?"

"No, though I taught for some while at the Colored Orphanage in New York, and set up my own school in South Carolina."

"Ah, that will explain the accent. I'm actually looking for a governess for my daughter. We live in Bath. It's just a short train ride away. A mere thirty minutes. Please take this. It's the money for the fare. Could you come to visit us Sunday afternoon? You could meet her and we could talk further. Let me tell you my address. As a teacher, I'm sure you must have a good memory for such things."

Mosa didn't quite know why she decided to go. Probably because it offered a chance to escape from the misery of factory work. The train journey was brief as he had said. Perhaps she would be able to make the journey there and back each day.

Bath was a revelation. Bristol had a wealthy quarter but this whole city appeared to be one of riches. Situated in a bowl and surrounded by steep hills of lush green, the grand houses were all constructed of the same stone, a soft honey color. The effect was charming. A place of calm and grace after the putrid slums of Bristol where Mosa lived and worked.

Asking directions, she made her way to the address which de Montfort had told her, number ten the Royal Crescent. As she turned the corner and saw the Crescent for the first time, she was in awe. A huge curve of architecture stretched for a considerable distance, thirty large townhouses fronted by Ionic columns. In front of them, across the cobbled street, lay a huge expanse of sloping lawn leading to a park. Fluffy white clouds scudded across the sapphire sky above.

It all spoke of a perfect world for those fortunate enough to live there. They would never have to see the England that most of the population inhabited, and they could believe their land was truly God's own country, a paradise on earth.

The maid opening the door was dressed in black with white lace around the neck. She looked taken aback to see a person of Mosa's color calling, even more so when she explained that she had an appointment with Mr. Edward who appeared from a side room to greet her.

"Thank you for coming. I trust your journey here was agreeable. I thought we could take tea in the garden as it is such a lovely day."

The maid's eyes looked as though they might pop out of their sockets with surprise that he should be entertaining this woman. She would certainly have some gossip to share with the other servants below stairs when they assembled for their meal this evening.

De Montfort cut a dashing figure with his head of thick black hair which touched his collar and his long sideburns which reached his jaw. His eyes were welcoming.

The garden was a riot of color. Well stocked flowerbeds grew up against the stone walls. Butterflies fluttered from one flower to another and bees hovered gathering nectar.

A young girl of about nine or ten with her hair in ringlets ran around the lawn, chasing a small dog as it wagged its tail and barked happily. She only glanced at Mosa for a moment before returning to her game.

"That's my daughter, Arabella. I'll introduce you to her later. Do please sit. So tell me, what has brought you to England?"

"My husband was a politician, a Republican Representative in the State Legislature in South Carolina. He was murdered by his opponents. I feared what would happen next so I decided to leave."

"I'm sorry. I have read of the violence. I have business interests in the United States and follow events there closely. You may have heard that the Democrats took the South and the Presidential election was very close and the result disputed. The Democrats agreed to allow the Republican candidate, Rutherford Hayes, to have the White House on the condition that Reconstruction be ended and Federal troops withdrawn, leaving the South to its own devices once more."

"No, I haven't been able to get news of America since coming here. You have confirmed my worst fears about what would happen. It's so sad, we had made so much progress."

"It seems you made a wise decision to leave. May we discuss what you would teach my daughter? I would be excited to have someone from your country teach her, and in due course Henry too.

People here don't realize it yet, but the future will be driven by the United States, not Britain. Last time I visited, I was astonished by how fast things are developing there."

"In the North maybe."

Before she had finished her cup of tea, Edward had offered her the job.

"Thank you. I'm happy to accept. What time do you want me here in the mornings?"

"You would live here."

"That wouldn't be possible. I have a ten year old boy and a six month old baby."

"They could live here too. Arabella loves babies, and Henry would benefit from a boy's company."

"Does Mrs. de Montfort agree?"

"Sadly she died giving birth to Henry."

Mosa decided to take the chance. It would be a much nicer environment for her children than their present squalid accommodation. Her main worry was how Lowenna would take it.

"Don't you worry about me. I'll be able to rent a smaller place. And I can come visit you in Bath on a Sunday sometimes. It'll be something to look forward to."

CHAPTER 23

Edward de Montfort's unconventional choice met with his mother's opposition. Mosa heard her shrill voice of protest clearly enough through a half open door.

"How can a half breed be a governess? She's not acquainted with English etiquette."

"I'm looking for an educator, not a finishing school. Arabella can have that when she's older."

His mother wasn't persuaded.

"Having an American would be bad enough, but her? What will others say?"

"Mother, she is a very accomplished lady, and so widely read. I think I'm lucky to have found her."

"Really? And what about that awful scar on her face. What does that say about her?"

"It says she's had to overcome adversity and hatred. Something which would have destroyed many lesser people. It speaks volumes about her strength of character."

"Well, get her to apply some rouge at the very least. And why on earth did you agree to her children living here? I swear you've lost all sense of reason, Edward. How do we even know she was ever a married woman? Have you forgotten who we are?"

"I have no doubt she is telling the truth. And as for who we are, no, I haven't forgotten. Not at all. We're a family whose wealth was derived from the slave trade, although I don't expect that is something which you boast about to your social circle."

Mosa looked up at the unsmiling portraits of ancestors on the walls of the hallway from where she was listening to the conversation. Like those which had once hung in the mansion at the Old Oaks Plantation, those portrayed to be the epitome of dignity and morality were nothing of the sort, complicit in human suffering and grown rich because of it.

Bristol had built much of its prosperity on the Triangular Trade. Ships departed for West Africa loaded with goods and returned with kidnapped Africans who were shipped to what were once the American colonies. The triangle was complete when the same ships returned from there with cotton and tobacco. The practice continued until 1807, even though slavery was ruled to be illegal in England in 1772.

Arabella was a diligent though not particularly smart student. Whilst Mosa was pleased to be teaching again, she missed the interaction that came from working with a class full of children.

The first night that Arabella's father went away,

Mosa was awakened by her door opening. Arabella stood there in her nightdress, flickering candle-light outlining her as though she was an apparition.

"Is something the matter?"

"I'm frightened being all alone in my bedroom, knowing I'm the only person on my floor. Please may I sleep on the floor next to you?"

"No, but you can hop in and sleep in my bed. But you must be quiet. We don't want to wake Maisie in her cot."

Mosa soon realized that the child wanted nothing more than to be mothered. Privileged she might be, yet without a mother's love she often appeared lost and unsure of herself. Mosa understood how she must feel, never having experienced a mother's love herself.

Arabella's father was frequently away on business, and her grandmother, being very much of the view that children should be seen and not heard, rarely spent any time with her. The girl became an adjunct to Mosa's family, passing her evenings up in Mosa's room while they read and played games.

As governess, Mosa wasn't expected to eat with the other servants and so was able to eat with her family and Arabella. The rest of the staff were distinctly cool toward the new arrival. Her informal "Hi, I'm Mosa" attracted little response other than sniffs of superiority.

Arabella and Thomas became good friends. They would sneak out of the back gate and go exploring together. They ignored the looks of disapproval which adults on the street often gave them, scandalized to see a white girl running about with someone who was black. One particular day they climbed the steep hills surrounding the city. When they reached the top, they wandered amongst a herd of cows. Some were noisily chewing the grass, others lay there impassively. Arabella poked one until it got up and moved.

"The grass is always nice and warm where they've been sitting. Try it."

They sat looking down at the streets far below, the dwellings like dolls houses from their vantage point.

"Why didn't your father come with you?"

"He died. He got shot."

"Did the police catch the man who did it?"

"It doesn't quite work like that where I'm from. Not if you're my color."

"Well, I think you're a beautiful color."

Embarrassed, Thomas occupied himself picking individual blades of grass.

"Have you ever kissed someone before?" asked Arabella.

"What kind of question is that?"

"That means you haven't. Neither have I. Shall we try, to see what it's like?"

"I..."

Arabella had already closed her eyes and pouted her lips. Hesitantly, Thomas put his lips against hers. They stayed like that for a few moments as if they were two statues. Arabella pulled away first.

"I can't see what all the fuss is about. Can you? We should be getting back. It'll be time for supper soon. Come on, I'll race you."

With the wind in their faces, they let out yells of delight as they ran down the slope until Thomas tripped and went head over heels. Spraining an ankle, he had to limp all the way home.

Lowenna often came to Bath on her day off. She and Mosa would stroll around the park. Leaves beginning to turn yellow hinted at the fast approaching change of season. Mosa didn't welcome the prospect of another six months of rain and gales, though at least this year the weather should be held at bay more effectively than where they had lived in Bristol.

"I received a proposal."

"Who from?" asked Mosa.

"Bill, he's a blacksmith."

"Did you accept?"

"No, I want to be there for Abe when he returns."

"Have you considered that he might never return?"

"Of course, but if he did I don't want him to feel rejected. I gave him a lot to deal with, not letting him know who he was. Marrying someone he doesn't know and has never met would likely make him leave again and not come back."

"You're a good mother, Lowenna. One day he's gonna appreciate that."

As Christmas approached, Edward de Montfort announced his intention to hold a ball.

"I'd like for you to come," he said to Mosa.

"I can't dance, at least not how a lady is expected to, and I don't have anything suitable to wear."

"Never fear, Mrs. Henderson the dressmaker who I use for Arabella will create something spectacular for you."

The blue silk shimmered like sunlight on water. Yet all the finery did nothing to lessen Mosa's anxiety. The night of the party she delayed, staying up in her room on the top floor like a hermit hiding from the world. But not to go would seem rude. Steeling herself, she slowly made her way down the stairs, all the while fighting the desire to go back up, a desire which increased the louder the undercurrent of chatter and laughter became as she approached the room.

Mosa had hoped she might slip in barely noticed. That her entrance caused conversations to halt mid-sentence and faces to turn in her direction as ladies positioned their fans in front of their mouths to whisper to each other, made Mosa want to turn and flee.

She was just about to do so when from across the room, Edward spotted her. Smiling broadly, he came to welcome her. He bowed and kissed her hand.

"If I may be so bold as to say so, you look positively radiant."

"I feel anything but."

"Ignore these inbreds. I care not one jot for their

opinions." He nodded at the quartet in one corner which began playing. "May I have the pleasure of this dance?"

"I already told you I can't."

"There's nothing to it. Trust me. Just take my hand and follow my lead."

As they danced a feeling of joy began building within her, crowding out the confidence sapping self-consciousness of earlier. They swirled around the room, forcing the onlookers to back against the walls to make space for them. Mosa felt a lightness as if she might fly as Edward twirled her round and round. The gawkers soon tired of watching them have fun and took to the floor themselves.

Mosa must have stopped dancing at some point - she remembered being faced with inane questions such as did she know where in Africa she was from - but it seemed like she had danced the night away when the ball ended. As she climbed the stairs, she couldn't help but smile to herself. She couldn't re-call when she had felt like this. The ropes of worry which had held her down for so long seemed broken.

The next time Mosa met Lowenna she could tell before they even spoke that her friend had re-ceived news. Her face positively shone with jubi-lation.

"He's written. He's in New Orleans."

"That's wonderful. When will he be back?"

"He won't. He's got a job on the Mississippi steamboats. I'm leaving. Going to New Orleans."

"Did he ask you to?"

"No, but I've no life here so I may as well be where my son is. It's far enough away from South Carolina that I won't have to worry about Thackery."

"I'll be sorry to see you go." And Mosa hoped Abraham would be pleased to see his mother. Yet to burst Lowenna's balloon with such a thought seemed cruel.

"I'll miss you as well. I'll write as soon as I get there. My boat goes in three days. I'm so excited."

After they had hugged, Mosa watched her depart, not moving until she was out of sight. Lowenna had become a dear friend but now she would never see her again. A melancholy wrapped Mosa in its cold embrace. Being a single mother was hard without the support of family and friends, and even more so in a foreign country.

On Christmas Day, Edward asked Mosa and her children to accompany him and his children to morning service. She had previously seen Bath Abbey from the outside but this was the first occasion on which she had entered. It was truly breathtaking with the fan vaulting on its high ceilings and bright stained glass windows. Yet the solemnity of the service didn't evoke for her the joy of the promise of an eternity without hate and sorrow.

Upon their return to the house, Edward had gifts not only for Arabella but for Mosa's children also. While they giggled with delight as they ripped off the paper, he asked Mosa if she would join him that evening and not to worry, his mother would be at his sister's all day long.

When she came down that night, it was like the perfect Christmas that she had always imagined. A roaring fire and a tree reaching to the ceiling, decked with small candles. A holly wreath hung above the mantlepiece, and the smell of pine and the smoke from his cigar created an aroma which she found most appealing.

"Merry Christmas, Mosa," he said, standing as she entered.

"And to you, Mr. de Montfort."

"Please call me Edward. I have a little something for you. Let me get it from under the tree."

He handed her a thin, dark blue box. Inside was a gold necklace.

"This is too much."

"Nonsense. I haven't seen Arabella this happy since before her mother died. I'm extremely grateful to you for that. Here, let me put it on for you." Mosa felt herself tremble a little as his hands brushed the skin on the back of her neck. "There's a mirror over there. Take a look. It complements your lovely skin tone perfectly."

"It's beautiful, thank you."

"Come sit down," he said, indicating the sofa where he sat down also.

Mosa perched herself on the edge, placing her hands on her lap.

"Mosa, there's something I wish to ask you. Since

you came here, you've transformed not only my daughter's life but mine too. I haven't felt this alive in ages."

He got up and went down on one knee before her.

"Would you do me the honor of becoming my wife?"

CHAPTER 24

Mosa opened her mouth, but no words would come. She had become uncomfortably hot.

"I can see that this is unexpected. I appreciate you need time to think. I leave tomorrow for London and will be gone for a week. Maybe you could give me your answer then, or take longer if you wish. As long as you need."

"No, I'll give you my answer when you return. I really should be getting back up in case Maisie wakes. Goodnight, Edward."

"Goodnight, Mosa."

He stood too. The warmth of Christmas was reflected in his eyes. However, she didn't seek to hold his gaze and departed in haste.

Up in her room as she fiddled with her necklace, she looked through the small window out into an obsidian world. Not once had she given the possibility a moment's consideration. She had never thought about marrying again, particularly not such a man as this.

The next day, she left Maisie with Thomas and went out for a walk. Thick snowflakes were falling from a leaden sky, decorating the top of the railings in the Crescent like cotton balls. For distraction Mosa stuck out her tongue to catch a snowflake, enjoying the cold as it dissolved.

Edward's proposal offered her and her children a comfortable life, a life of no worries about where the money to pay rent or buy food would come from. Yet at what cost? Would her children resent her one day for living here in this often stifling English upper class atmosphere, turning them into minor aristocrats and denying their heritage? They would always stand out, be a thing apart. Who would ever truly accept them other than Edward?

And what would her life become? Probably one of being there when required, a decoration to adorn his arm at social functions. Reduced to an exotic curiosity. She didn't believe that was Edward's intention, but that would be the outcome. The wife of a Victorian gentleman most certainly wasn't expected to have a career or ambition of her own. Her role was ordained to be one of supporting her husband as he wished to be supported.

Maybe such concerns could be overcome, a way forward found. But what would Mosa be doing if she didn't marry for love? Edward was a man with many admirable qualities, however she didn't love him. She liked him and enjoyed his company. That was as far as it went.

However, turn him down and they'd have to leave. What future then for her children? Perhaps she would grow to love him. She wanted safety and security for Thomas and Maisie. Marrying Edward would give them that.

Mosa had reached the Circus, an enclave of magnificent Georgian townhouses built to form a large circle, broken only for the three street entrances. In the circular patch of grass in the middle under the trees which no longer looked forlorn now snow gilded their bare branches, she made her decision. She couldn't decide. In a few days she would need to, but for now she didn't have to.

Those intervening days passed in a blur. Mosa didn't live in the moment. Her mind had been taken hostage. At times it soared with visions of laughter and smiles, of balls and Christmas trees. A life of abundance. At other times it fell, dragged down deep by chains. Chains of conformity and not being free to be true to herself.

When Edward returned, Mosa waited until he was in his study. Her heart beat more loudly than her delicate knock. Her life was about to change forever.

"Come in."

Seeing her, he leaped to his feet.

"Ah, Mosa. I have missed your company."

"Edward, I have reached my decision."

"Oh."

There was a nervous anticipation in his voice.

"I must respectfully decline your proposal."

Edward couldn't hide his disappointment as the expectant smile he wore dissolved in the ripples of her refusal.

"I appreciate that it would be a huge change for you. Is there anything that I can say to alter your mind?"

"I'm afraid not."

"May I ask why?"

"I'm not cut out for your life. It's not who I am. Nor do I think it would be the right thing to do for Thomas and Maisie. One day, I would like to return to America. Teach in a school, maybe found my own even. Many children there get so little education and some none at all. It's education that could change their lives, I truly believe that. Meanwhile, I'll look for new employment, and we'll be gone just as soon as you've found a new teacher for Arabella."

"No, please don't do that. There's no need."

So Mosa stayed. Edward de Montfort remained the perfect gentleman, always courteous when they met, though that was infrequently. He traveled more and spent much of his time at his London home.

Mosa saved what she could. She wanted to get back to South Carolina where Thomas and Maisie could be with children like them. In a couple of years she should have enough to go.

Some months passed. She awoke each morning to birdsong. Leaves appeared on the trees in the garden in the fresh bright green of spring. Life was easy but unchallenging and uninspiring.

Coming in one day with Arabella, Mosa almost

bumped into Edward leaving as she pushed open the heavy door.

"Oh, I'm so sorry," said Mosa, though her thoughts had already turned to wondering who was the lady accompanying him in the large hat sprouting almost as many feathers as an ostrich.

"Not at all, Mosa. It was my fault for lurking behind the door. May I introduce you to Lady Isadora Smythe-Forsyth."

"Ah, the famous governess."

Her tone was condescending, as viscous as oil.

"Pleased to meet you, Ma'am."

"I've heard so much about you. You're practically a legend in your own time." She gave a little high pitched squeak of a laugh. "And what a ravishing beauty you are."

Her words hung uncomfortably between them.

"Well, we must be off or we'll miss our train. Come Isadora. I'll see you next week, Arabella. Be a good girl."

Mosa and Arabella stood back to let them pass.

"I don't like her," said Arabella.

"I'm sure you will when you get to know her."

"I doubt it. I do hope Papa doesn't marry her. I wish he'd marry you instead."

"My, whatever gave you such a notion."

CHAPTER 25

It wasn't long after that encounter until Mosa was summoned to Edward's study. Something clearly was troubling him as he paced around the room, his head down and his hand on his chin, consumed by his thoughts. Mosa stood at the door waiting for him to notice her.

"Ah Mosa, please do come on in." He didn't ask her to sit so she remained standing. "I have some news. Lady Isadora and I are to be married."

"Congratulations. I'm very happy for you."

"Thank you. It will mean there will be some changes I'm afraid. She…I mean I, think it would be best if you were to leave."

"I understand."

"I'm very grateful for all that you've done. I have a little something here for you. To help you with your school plans."

He handed her an envelope which lay on his desk. Her name was written in a bold flourish.

"Thank you, that's very kind. How soon would you like us to leave? When you find a new governess?"

DAVID CANFORD

"We won't be looking for another one. Arabella will be going to boarding school. She's old enough now, and it will do her good to mix with others her own age."

Mosa felt sorry for the girl. The English upper classes had an odd attitude to their children. They educated them at home without social interaction with their peers, then threw them in at the deep end by shipping them off to a school far from home so that they saw their parents even less than before. Character building, they called it.

"When will she be going?"

"In September, but there's no need for you to stay until then. I have made inquiries about sailings for Charleston. There's a ship leaving Bristol this very evening. I've taken the liberty of booking your passage. It's all paid for. Your train departs in a couple of hours. Jones will take you all to the station in my carriage."

"May I say goodbye to Arabella?"

"She's out for the day with her grandmother. I thought it best not to upset her with goodbyes."

"Oh." Mosa wanted to see her and wish her well. Now the poor girl would be left thinking Mosa didn't care, that Arabella's trust in her had been betrayed. "May I write to her? I fear she may think badly of me for leaving without saying anything."

"There's no need. I've already handled it. Well, you'd better go pack. Goodbye, Mosa. I'm glad to have known you."

He put his hand out to shake hers.

"You too, Edward."

Mosa wasn't surprised that his new wife to be didn't want her there, even if she was taken aback by how quickly they were to depart. She would, however, be going home which is what she wanted.

From the carriage, Mosa took her last look at the streets of Bath. It was indeed a handsome place, but she had no regrets. It wasn't home and never would have been.

Once on the train, she opened the envelope Edward had given her. Inside was a money order for three hundred pounds. Fifteen hundred dollars at the then exchange rate, a large sum of money at the time.

Mosa was thankful. She need no longer have any worries about how they would manage when they got back. More than that, she could start the school that she dreamed of.

The hope of true freedom for all may be squashed for now, but ever the optimist she believed one day in the not too distant future it would come. And it would be through education that the next generation would be able to get their chance, of that she was convinced. Mosa planned to set up somewhere near Old Oaks Plantation. She couldn't help but grin as she imagined their happy faces, their laughter, and how wonderful it would be to hug old friends. Through teaching she would give their children the means with which to escape their parents' lives.

Sadly, Mosa's optimism proved to be misplaced. The end of Reconstruction made it easier to exclude black voters from the electoral process, and eventually new laws would be passed in the Southern States to legalize that exclusion, laws which would last nearly a hundred years until the Voting Rights Act of 1965.

The crossing was uneventful. On the morning of their arrival she left Thomas and Maisie sleeping and went on deck, excited to watch their entry into Charleston harbor. It was blissful to breathe in that warm heat of morning after nearly two years away. Eager to get off as soon as the ship docked, she woke the children to ensure that they were the first to disembark.

"And just where do you think you're going?"

A voice as hard as granite came from a man in a dark uniform and peak cap, a port official of some kind.

"We're going to the station to take a train to Columbia."

"Really. And where did you board?"

"England."

"Well, we don't need more niggers here, we've enough of our own."

"I'm not English. We've just been away for a while."

"Makes no difference. If you want to reside here, you'll need a white person to post a bond to guarantee your good behavior."

"I don't understand."

"Since you've been gone, there's been some changes. We have a proper government now. One that maintains decency and public order. It's not an unruly free for all like before."

"But I was born here."

"Well, you can insist on staying and maybe I can't stop you, but your son would most probably be entered into an apprenticeship. Placed with a white family that needs help and your daughter too, in somebody's care until she is old enough to work."

"Why?"

"Because you're as good as a vagrant. Now why don't you get back on that ship and save us all some trouble."

"It's going to New Orleans."

"You'll have to choose. If you don't decide in the next minute, I'll summon the police and you'll be incarcerated while they decide what to do with you. I'd go if I were you. And I'll give you another piece of free advice. Instead of coming off first next time and standing around in full view, hide amongst the crowd. That way you're less likely to be noticed."

Mosa's breathing was fast and shallow. She thought briefly of making a dash for it, but Maisie couldn't run, and even if she carried her they'd surely be caught. There was no choice. She couldn't risk her children being taken away from her.

"Come on kids, let get back on."

Still in a state of disbelief at what was happening, Mosa watched Charleston grow smaller until it was only a memory. She wondered how could it have come to this. An exile in her own country. She knew nothing of New Orleans. And what if they received the same treatment there?

Returning to England didn't appeal and she didn't know where else she could go. Africa wasn't hers. Her skin was too pale and her parents weren't black. Once again she would stand out, her children less so, but even they were clearly of mixed race. Mosa wondered if it was to be her destiny to wander the globe, always searching. Searching for a place of acceptance and safety. For her children's sake, she masked her anxieties.

"What an adventure we're having. I've heard New Orleans is a wonderful city. You're lucky to see so much of the world. Some folk stay stuck in the same place all their lives never knowing what's over the next hill."

"I don't want to see the world. I want to go back home and see my friends like you promised," complained Thomas.

"You'll make new friends."

"I don't want to. If we'd never left, none of this would've happened."

Thomas threw off her arm from around his shoulder and walked along the deck. Maisie gripped her mother's hand tightly, looking up at her with doleful eyes seeking reassurance and not understanding any of what was going on.

CHAPTER 26

Several more days passed until they approached a coastline which seemed to be neither ocean nor land, only a maze of both. The sea turned from blue to an alluvial brown. Passing low lying swampland, they entered the mouth of the Mississippi.

A hundred miles upriver the ship reached New Orleans, perched on a crescent shaped bend and sitting on a natural levee. With a population of around two hundred thousand, it was four times larger than Charleston. An eclectic mix of ships and steamboats lined the waterfront. The sight of them finally cheered up Thomas.

"Look at that one with the big wheel. I want to go on that."

"I'm sure you will one day, son. Right now, I need you to do as we discussed. When I say so we get off and, remember, no dawdling. Keep your head down and follow me and Maisie. We don't want to draw attention to ourselves."

Letting others disembark first, the area by the ship was already crowded when they came down the gangplank. Mosa marched her children quickly away from the wharf, all the while dreading hearing that shout to stop, like a lasso around her waist pulling her back. But no challenge came.

Once on the city sidewalks, they slowed. The air was heavy, weighed down with moisture, making their clothes cling to them as if they had just climbed out of the Mississippi itself. The intensity of the humidity was considerably higher than South Carolina.

They reached an area of architecture pleasing to the eye with elaborate and intricate ironwork encasing balconies from which the inhabitants languidly observed the passing world below. At the far end of one street stood a church, the likes of which Mosa had never seen before. In the center a tower topped by a conical roof shaped like a giant wizard's hat reached for the sky, complemented by ones at either end of the building's frontage.

"Is that a castle for a princess?" asked Maisie.

"Maybe. We shall go see one day."

The place didn't look American or feel it. Around them, some spoke in a language Mosa didn't understand. They were in the Vieux Carré, the French Quarter, and oldest part of town. The last bastion of the dwindling number of French speakers, Creoles, descended from the original colonial inhabitants after France established La Nouvelle-Orléans in 1718.

Unlike other cities in the South, New Orleans hadn't suffered heavy bombardment and the consequent destruction. The Union had taken it in 1862, keen to block the Confederacy's access into and out of the Mississippi. Once forts downriver had been captured, the taking of the city itself had proved straightforward.

Although in the South, New Orleans wasn't Southern in the way of other Southern States. Its history had been different, and the local accent wasn't the Southern drawl. It almost sounded as if the locals were from Brooklyn, New York.

The mix of people was noticeably different too. There were people of every shade of skin color. So many were of mixed race compared to South Carolina. As Mosa was to discover, it was a true melting pot.

Mosa found them a place to rent in Tremé, the black neighborhood just north of the French Quarter. At first sight there was little to recommend it. A district of wooden shacks and dusty roads. The cobblestones didn't stretch beyond the French Quarter. When it rained, as it did almost every day preceded by spectacular fork lightning and thunderclaps louder than they had ever heard, the uneven mud road became a place of deep puddles for the adults to navigate around. For the children they were a welcome diversion, something to jump in or over.

Not a single building in this faubourg, as the city's different areas were referred to, appeared to contain a right angle. Several leaned precariously as if a hurricane must recently have passed through, though that wasn't the case. Tremé had the worn, torn look of somebody who had labored in the cotton fields their entire life and could barely stand come evening. Yet despite appearances, there was vitality and vibrancy amongst its inhabitants.

Out on the streets, Thomas soon made new friends, and his truculence at having to come to New Orleans was cast aside. He was free to explore as never before.

Beyond Tremé lay the Backswamp, a wilderness on his doorstep which dissolved into the vast waters of Lake Pontchartrain to the north. It was a place where a child's imagination could run wild. Adults' warnings to stay out were disregarded by him and his friends.

Armed with sticks in case they should meet the snakes or alligators which they had been told would kill them, the children would wade through the shallow waters of the swamp which had the consistency of pea soup. The odor of decay they barely noticed. They had more important things on their mind as they acted out their fantasies, pretending to be pirates or African warriors.

In years to come, the Backswamp would be drained for housing. As it dried out and ceased to be an absorbent sponge, the land sank below sea level, exposing the city to the flooding which nature had once helped to protect it from.

One afternoon Thomas returned, carrying a white egg as though it were as valuable as a Fabergé owned by the Czar of Russia.

"Just what do you have there?" demanded his mother.

"We took it from a gator's nest."

"Did you now. Well, you know you're not supposed to go in the swamp. You need to take it back."

"Oh, please Mom let me keep it, just until it hatches."

"Please let him," added Maisie, hoping to be allowed to hold it.

"OK, just this once."

Brother and sister spent a great deal of their time during the following days clutching the egg close to keep it warm, and wrapping it in a blanket when they had to go out. One day, it began to crack. Fascinated, they watched as the baby alligator broke free. It seemed so cute with its big eyes and small body, like a toy dinosaur almost.

They filled a bucket with water and let the alligator lie in there when they were busy or sleeping. The rest of the time, they would lift it out and crawl about after it as it explored their cabin. They christened it Al. They had assumed its gender, not knowing how to determine otherwise.

Asking around as to what to feed Al, they gathered snails and insects, and Thomas and his friends brought back some small fish from the swamp. Children from streets around came to see their wondrous pet. It wasn't long before it began to grow.

"That creature must go," insisted Mosa. "I do not want to come home one day and be unable to find my children and see a big fat gator with a big ole grin on its face."

Followed by a procession of other children, Thomas carried the bucket as Maisie imperiously led the way to the swamp's edge. Al no longer fitted in the bucket and lay with his head resting on the top of it. As solemn as though they were attending a burial, they tipped Al into the water. In a flash of his tail he was gone, into the reeds and lost to them forever.

"I hope he finds his family," said Thomas.

"But we were his family."

"Yes, Sis, we were for a little while, but he'll be happier this way. He's free now like everyone should be." Seeing her face crumple, he added, "Come on, jump on my back and I'll give you a ride home."

Mosa went to visit the local school. It was nothing more than a one room shack. Angelique, the Creole teacher, was supportive of her plans. She was from a family who had lived in the city longer than they could recall. Part French, part African and part Choctaw, Angelique had inherited angular facial features.

"We do the best we can here, but as you can see it's overcrowded and under resourced. We can only take children for a couple of years maximum. Most leave us without a decent grasp of the basics. "The city authorities ain't the least bit interested in giving us more. Their view is that for the jobs these kids should in their opinion be doing, reading and writing isn't necessary. It's also easier for the white bosses to take advantage when our folk can't understand what they're signing, or do the math to question how little they're being paid, or challenge the arbitrary deductions taken off what they're owed. So they remain trapped in poverty with no opportunity to make something of themselves."

When she spoke, the Gallic influence came to the fore as Angelique raised her hands and threw them outward like a preacher. Mosa was fascinated by her long and slender fingers which emphasized each point she made.

"Will you be offering evening classes? A lot of the older kids have to work during the day. It's the teenagers that need that extra bit of learning."

"I'd be happy to if I could find someone to keep an eye on my young daughter," said Mosa.

"Well, I could help you out there. And there's really no need to be thinking about having a schoolhouse of your own. This one's empty every evening, and it won't cost you nothing."

Mosa and Angelique passed word around. The first evening Mosa arrived to teach, the line of youngsters stretched around the corner. Few had shoes on their feet and many weren't dressed in a lot more than rags, but their faces were witness to their eagerness. It was raining heavily, though on a lethargic New Orleans day the warm raindrops were a welcome event. Inside, jets of water cascaded through holes in the roof. Already soaked through, no one paid any attention to it. When all were in there, it was standing room only.

"I'm so glad Y'all came, but as you can see it's a little crowded in here so I'm gonna walk around and tell you number one or two. If you're a one then please come Mondays and Wednesdays, and twos, you should come Tuesdays and Thursdays. If you can't make your day, then you need to swap with somebody."

After the first couple of weeks attendance did drop off, but there were still about twenty children who came each night.

One evening after the children left, Samuel one of the older boys remained behind. Already well over six feet tall, he towered over his classmates. He was so thin, it seemed likely that a strong gust of wind would surely topple him.

"Time to go, Samuel. I gotta close up and get home now."

"Miss, would you be able to give me some private coaching? I could pay you. I've decided I want to become an attorney to fight for justice. I need help with the entrance exam."

"Well, that's an admirable ambition and I'd love to help you, but how would you afford the tuition fees for college? Would they let you in even if you could?"

"Yes. There's Straight University, it's for colored folk. They offer scholarships. I intend to qualify for one by being the best student."

"It's a deal then, but I don't want to be paid. How long until the exams?"

"Almost a year."

"That'll soon pass. Can you come to class one hour early?"

"Yes."

"OK, we'll make a start tomorrow."

Mosa was enthused with a passion once more. Helping people like Samuel to achieve was what would in time enable the status quo to be challenged.

She found a three room single story place in reasonably good repair to buy for a hundred dollars. It was near Congo Square, where Tremé and the French Quarter rub shoulders. Mosa was so happy to be giving her family a home of their own at last. No longer would they be nomads. She was content that fate had brought them here. It felt like a place they could settle.

Although white supremacy had been re-established by intimidation and electoral fraud as elsewhere in the former Confederate States, they couldn't squash the enthusiasm for life of New Orleans' underclass. The history of French and Spanish colonialism and African slaves, the iconography of Catholicism, and the mystery of Voodoo had all percolated the city with a joie de vivre and a sensuality repressed on the Protestant East Coast.

Music was all pervasive. At times, it felt as if the

rickety wooden planks of the sidewalks themselves must be the keys of a giant old piano. Rare was the time that you didn't hear someone somewhere creating music. From kids using washboards and kazoos to the marching bands, or a solitary trumpet blowing as the moon hung over the city like a giant paper lantern.

Congo Square itself was a center for spontaneous music and dancing. In French colonial times, free Africans and slaves on their then mandated day off on a Sunday used to gather to celebrate their heritage. When the United States assumed control, they eventually put a stop to it. With their right to vote effectively ended by threats of violence against those who might dare to do so, and proposed laws to disenfranchise them, African Americans turned once again to music as a way of expressing themselves and giving voice to how they felt with all other avenues now closed to them.

When the old lady next door died, Mosa got to experience her first New Orleans funeral. One of the local brass bands with slow mournful music accompanied the cortege as they cried out their lamentations. Once her body was "let loose", the band and those following broke into unrestrained, uptempo joy. Women twirled parasols and men threw their hats in the air as they all found release from the bleakness that their daily life could be.

Come February, there was the highlight of the city's year, Mardi Gras, a decidedly unAmerican event. Both Thomas and Maisie were enthralled by the extravagant floats of Rex, the king, and others. There were masked revelers, torchbearers, jugglers, and marching bands. A chaotic commotion of celebration, living up to its name of the greatest free show on earth. No one slept much or worked for that matter during the festival, there was too much fun to be had.

Mosa made Native American costumes for her children to parade in as part of the African Americans' salute to the original inhabitants of Louisiana. A tribute from those whose ancestors had been forced to come here to those who had been forced off their land.

CHAPTER 27

When Thomas wasn't running around Tremé or wading through the Backswamp, he would often head down to the "Big Muddy" to watch the steamboats come and go. While most carried cargo up and down the liquid highway to the interior, some took passengers heading up river to Natchez, Memphis, St Louis and the stops in between. With more than a little envy, Thomas would watch the well-heeled white clientele step aboard, serenaded by a band as he daydreamed about how one day he too would watch the city bid him a musical goodbye.

Mosa noticed that the boy seemed to have an innate talent for music. Kneeling on the ground and surrounded by his collection of gourds, he could attract a crowd as he beat out a rhythm. For his thirteenth birthday, she gave him a second hand trumpet and arranged for Old Man Joe down the street to give him lessons.

With his straw hat and a face which contained more lines than the Mississippi delta itself, Thomas decided the man must be a least a hundred years old even if he told the ladies that he was only thirty-nine and available for love. Whatever Joe's true age, he could make a trumpet sing like no one else. Lucky to be taught by a master, Thomas made good progress, and it wasn't any months until he got invited to join one of the marching bands.

It was soon after that Mosa finally got around to trying to get in touch with Lowenna. Not knowing if she'd still be in the city, Mosa set out one Sunday afternoon armed with the last address she had for her. She smiled when she found the street in the French Quarter. All this time they had been living less than a mile apart.

It wasn't Lowenna who answered the door. A strong smell of perfume from inside wafted onto the sidewalk.

"If you're looking for work girl, we ain't got none. And dressed like that, you'd have to pay some John to take it."

The lady dispensing the unwelcome advice was extravagantly dressed in the brightest of reds and a white feather boa.

"I've quite clearly got the wrong address. Goodbye."

Mosa's tone was sharp as a blade, offended by the woman's assumption. As she reached the corner, she ran right into Lowenna coming from the opposite direction.

"Lowenna, hi."

Her friend's expression wasn't one of happiness to

see her again. She put her head down and walked on.

"Wait. It's me, Mosa. Please stop. I only wanted to talk to you."

Lowenna halted and turned. Beneath her heavy makeup, her once lustrous green eyes appeared to have become opaque, no longer a window to her soul but a barrier of protection against what they now had to see.

"You wouldn't want to talk to me if you knew what I've become."

"I believe I already know. I'm not here to judge you," said Mosa putting her hand on Lowenna's arm. "We all do what we gotta do to survive. I've been lucky. I've had choices. Not everybody gets to choose. How's Abe keeping?"

"I don't know. We had a falling out. He refuses to talk to me. Still on the steamboats as far as I know."

"I'm sorry. We live here too now, in Tremé. Hey, you should come round for dinner some evening. I'm finished teaching by seven. What day can you make?"

"I don't think I can."

"Come on, there must be at least one."

"Tuesday then."

"Great, I'm only fifteen minutes from here. I wrote my address down before I came on this note in case you were out. Here, take it."

"I've got to go now."

"OK, see you Tuesday and don't forget. I'll cook

you something special."

Lowenna never showed up. Mosa decided to respect her wish to stay away and didn't seek to contact her again. She would remember Lowenna as she wanted to be remembered, for who she was before she had come to New Orleans.

Mosa and Angelique became close friends. They organized events to raise funds for the school and some money to pay Mosa for her efforts as that which Edward de Montfort had given was beginning to run out. Now approaching forty, Mosa felt old and frumpy next to her friend who was only in her early twenties.

Angelique taught her how to cook the New Orleans way. Mosa became expert at jambalayas, gumbos, and her children's favorite, beignets. The mere smell of them was guaranteed to make them come running home even from way down the street.

When Thomas became fifteen, Mosa decided that it was time to have a serious talk with him. Though he could read and write, he wasn't the academic kind. Yet he still needed to do something and was showing absolutely no inclination to look for proper work.

"You really need to get a job, son. Playing music is great but that's just a hobby which ain't gonna feed you and clothe you as you get older."

"I don't agree. I'm often being asked to help out now in the clubs when a trumpet player doesn't show. I made fifty cents last week."

"Fifty cents. You've gotta have more ambition than that."

"Music is all I care about."

"Well, you better start caring about finding some work. I'm tired of having to nag you about it. You've got a month, or you'll have to leave. If you wanna be lazy, you can do that someplace else."

"You don't mean that."

"No, Mama, don't throw Tommy out," piped up Maisie, who as a five year old worshipped the ground which her brother walked upon.

"I don't say things I don't mean. It's for your own good. I wouldn't be a good mother if I didn't stop your lollygagging. You were born free, a precious gift my generation were denied, so use that freedom and do something with your life."

"I'll go right now then."

In a temper, Thomas grabbed his trumpet, slamming the door shut as he left.

"Go get him," pleaded his sister.

"No, he's got to learn. But don't you worry, he'll be back by nightfall."

Mosa wished that Joshua was still with them. It was so tough raising a family alone. She worried that Thomas, lacking a male role model, would make bad choices. And more than that, she still missed Joshua.

CHAPTER 28

Thomas went down to the wharves as he had so many times before. A steamboat was discharging its passengers as the onboard band played. Once the last person had disembarked, the band did too carrying their shiny brass instruments.

"Hey, sir."

"You again? You sure are persistent," said the band leader, a rotund, short man who waddled from side to side as he walked. His cheeks were reminiscent of a chipmunk's as if he never succeeded in exhaling all the air that he had inhaled for blowing his tuba. However, Thomas had seen him perform and knew the man could belt it out like nobody, even if the instrument looked as though it ought to overwhelm a person of his size.

"Could you just listen to me play?"

"No need. I saw you at Ruby's a few weeks back. I know you can play."

"Well, could you hire me, give me a chance? Please, mister. I'm not worried about the money."

"Ain't no good if you were. Food and accommodation are included, and we get tips which we share out according to age and experience. You'd lose on both counts. But if you're still interested, come back here early tomorrow. You might just be in luck. Our trumpet player is sick. I'm not sure he'll be well enough to get back on."

"Oh, thank you, thank you."

"What's your name?"

"Thomas Elwood."

"Art, Art Croyde."

Propelled by hope and leaping into the air with unrestrained elation every so often, Thomas ran most of the way home.

"I thought you'd return," said Mosa when she got back from teaching that evening to find Thomas practicing his trumpet. "I meant what I said though."

Mosa didn't like the thought of having to go through with her threat, but she'd been pushing him to find work for some while now without any result.

"I may have a job. I find out for definite tomorrow."

"Well, congratulations. I'm proud of you, son. What is it?"

"In a band, on a steamboat that goes to St Louis."

"A steamboat?"

"Yeah, wouldn't it be great? I've always wanted to travel up and down the river."

"Yes, I guess so." Mosa hid the sadness which she felt inside. She hadn't considered that his work might take him away from here. But it would be a good experience for him and was likely to make him more mature. "I hope you're successful. When would you go?"

"In the morning. It heads back up river then."

"My, that's soon. Me and Maisie better come down so we can wave you off."

Art gave Thomas an affirmative nod as he arrived. Mosa kissed him. Maisie refused his attempt to hug her, sulking that her brother was leaving.

"Cheer up Maisie, I'll be back in a couple of weeks. I gotta go now. Bye."

Art greeted him as he embarked.

"Welcome aboard. Follow me while I introduce you to the captain so he don't think you're a stow-away. Then I'll take you down and we'll get you a uniform."

Their quarters were on the lowest deck. The smell from the livestock, which also traveled on it, was strong. It was cramped and basic but none of that bothered Thomas whose big adventure was about to begin.

Art gave him a white shirt, red vest and bow tie, and black pants, like the other band members wore.

"That's better. And shine those shoes. There's polish over there." As Thomas did so, Art briefed him. "Mainly we just play when they're getting off and on, and in the evenings. The rest of the time we gotta stay down here. You'll start on one percent of our takings."

Thomas had no idea how much that might be and

he didn't care. He was getting to do the thing which he loved best on the vessel that he'd wanted to travel on from the very first time he'd set eyes on a steamboat the day when he and his family had arrived in New Orleans.

"Let's go up on deck while we practice a little before the first guests arrive," said Art.

Thomas experienced such a thrill as the vessel emitted shrill, sharp hoots and belched black smoke from her two red funnels. Her paddle wheel began turning and she moved away from her mooring. Back down on their deck, he spent most of the day leaning over the rail watching the world glide by. They stuck mainly to the middle, and it was only when they veered toward one side or another that he could observe the land in detail.

Where the land had been tamed, there was the occasional antebellum mansion set far back in large grounds. More commonly the view was of shotgun shacks. Laughing children would run along the bank waving until they tired. Log rafts bobbed about close to the riverbank, maneuvered by pole. Most were small but a few were large, some even with a tent rigged up for accommodation. Cargo steamboats loaded with cotton bales or grain from the interior chugged by, bound for the ships waiting in New Orleans which would sail off to New York or England.

His bandmates were old hands who'd spent several years already going up and down Old Man

River. The others played a clarinet, saxophone, and trombone.

In years gone by, settlers had sailed down the Mississippi to carve out new lives and amass riches from the labor of the slaves accompanying them in chains. Now railroads offered a quicker means of travel. Today, it was the wealthy with plenty of time to spare who took the trip. The first class deck provided the level of comfort which they expected.

That first evening, Thomas was spellbound by the grandeur when they went up to perform. It was a world away from a couple of decks down. Mirrors reflected large chandeliers. Persian rugs and other sumptuous furnishings and fabrics adorned the palatial room. Never had he been in a place quite like this.

It was so different from the sweat and barely concealed passion infusing the venues he had played in back in the city. Here the audience sat at their tables in silence. If they moved at all to the music, it was usually in an awkward, uptight way that ended with an admonishing look from a spouse, or tap of a hand to calm down. The applause was brief and polite. No foot stomping, no hollers or shrieks for more as he was used to.

Thomas could barely sleep the first night, entranced by watching the reflection of a full moon dance on the water as fish jumped, attracted by its light.

The following day, he was glad to see a familiar

face in the smart navy blue uniform of an officer down on his deck. He'd become a man since Thomas had last seen him several years ago. His jaw was squarer but his freckles were just as numerous. He breezed straight past Thomas.

"Hey, Abe. It's me, Thomas. Don't you remember me? How are you doing?"

The man turned and walked up to him until he was so close to his face Thomas could smell his stale breath. Abraham's eyes narrowed.

"Sure, I know who you are. I know everything that happens on board. And if I'd wanted to talk to you, I would have done so already. Now listen, and listen real good. Don't you ever shout out at me like that again, or I'll have you thrown off at the next stop and chuck your stupid trumpet in the Mississippi. You don't ever, and I mean ever, talk to a white person on this boat unless they address you first. Understand?"

Thomas looked at him without replying.

"You'd better answer me, boy."

"Yes, sir."

Abraham spat. His spit landed on the floor, only narrowly missing Thomas' pants and shoes. He then promptly left the deck.

"Don't take it personally," said Art who had witnessed the encounter. "That mother is a mean one. I'd stay out of his way if I were you. Things might feel like they ought to be different out here on the river, but they ain't. Not one bit."

CHAPTER 29

Come the colder winter months, there wasn't the demand for travel on the river so the band stayed in New Orleans looking for gigs. The best paid were weddings and parties over in the Garden District. Less than two miles from Tremé, Thomas's first function there was also his first visit. If you weren't white, you didn't go to that part of town, not unless you worked for a family there. Substantial houses, which declared the wealth of those who lived there, stood on tree-lined avenues, another world to the poverty of Tremé.

Thomas also found part-time work hefting cargo down by the river. Mosa was impressed by her son's transformation. Her boy was growing into a fine young man. A handsome one too, with his mother's engaging eyes and his father's enchanting smile which had so captivated Mosa all those years ago.

One May evening as Mosa was sitting sewing, there was a knock on her door.

"Come on in."

The door opened only slowly as if the visitor was

uncertain whether Mosa's cheerful tone would alter once she saw who it was.

"Hello. I know I'm a little late for that dinner."

"You can say that again. I had to eat the entire gumbo that I'd made myself. I blame you for all this weight I'm putting on these days." laughed Mosa.

"You're not mad at me?"

"No, Lowenna. I'm just glad that you finally came. Sit down, we've got a lot of catching up to do." Her friend settled herself into a dining chair next to Mosa's. "Take that needle on the table can you and help me darn this pile of socks."

Lowenna did as requested.

"Are you and Abe speaking again?"

"No. Not sure we ever will."

"Why? Surely, things can't be that bad."

"I'm afraid they are. He got into debt gambling and came seeking my help. Said some men had threatened to kill him if he didn't pay. I didn't have enough so I borrowed. I told him he must promise me to stop gambling. We got into an argument, but I still gave him the money. I was frightened he'd end up dead otherwise. He took it and I haven't seen or heard from him since.

"My job as a chambermaid didn't pay enough to repay the loan sharks. They turned nasty, so... well, you've seen what I do."

They talked long into the evening until even the street outside had become silent.

"It's late, I really should be going," said Lowenna.

"You know if you wanted to get away from where you're at right now, you can always stay here while you get back on your feet again."

"I appreciate the offer, but you don't need to worry about me. My life's OK, really it is."

"Well, just make sure you come back soon."

As time passed, Thomas' share of tips grew. He had become the most accomplished member of the band. Like Old Man Joe, he could make that trumpet sound like few others could.

It had been over two years since he had first started on the river, but he never got tired of watching it roll by or seeing the towns they called at, even if he wasn't permitted to get off to explore them.

During the previous winter, he had picked up a new style of playing that was coming out of the streets. He tried to get Art to incorporate it into the band's repertoire, but he wasn't impressed.

"What you're doing has no real tune. How are folk ever gonna sing along or tap their feet to it?"

"They hardly ever do on this boat."

"Well, regardless of that, it's never the same twice."

"That's the whole idea. You improvise. It makes every performance unique. Each member of the band plays off the others, you all kinda inspire each other."

"Look, I've been doing this stuff since before you were born, and I know I'm right when I say it'll never catch on. Folk want what they know, music they feel comfortable with. If we played what you want us to, we'd be fired."

As the sun dipped giving a warm and golden glow to the landscape one evening, Thomas stood playing his trumpet on the lower deck. After a while he sensed that he was being watched. He stopped and looked to his side.

"Please don't stop. I love the way you play." The young woman's voice was as lovely as a harp. Hair the color of the evening light fell beyond her shoulders, and there was a sweet innocence to her gaze that could make a heart ache. Thomas was immediately smitten.

"Are you lost? Shouldn't you be up a few decks?"

"I was, on the upper deck, leaning over the side watching the sunset, then I heard you playing and I just had to come down. You play so beautifully."

Thomas felt a joy surge through him that his talent could have attracted her to come searching for him.

"What would you like to hear?"

"Anything, I don't mind."

He chose the most romantic melody he knew. As he played, he imagined them dancing together under the stars. When he finished, she clapped enthusiastically.

"Thank you. That was so pretty. My name's Emily."

"Thomas."

"Pleased to meet you, Thomas. I'm traveling back to New Orleans with my parents."

"That's where I'm from too."

"Maybe you could come and play for my eighteenth birthday party."

"Sure, I'd love to. Just tell me when and where."

"It's-"

"Miss, you shouldn't be down here. It's not a suitable place for a young lady such as yourself." Thomas recognized the unwelcome, rasping tone of Abraham, a man he rarely saw and who had never spoken to him since that first voyage. "Come, let me escort you back up."

"It's been so nice to meet you, Thomas. I hope we get to talk more before we reach New Orleans."

Emily gave him a bright smile. Abraham scowled.

"Hey, don't go getting any ideas," said Art, observing the far away look in Thomas' eyes as she left. "She's white, you're not. It ain't never gonna happen."

Thomas experienced a deep frustration, an excitement caged by anger. Emily made his heart beat faster, awakened a hunger in his soul which he didn't know he had, yet he was expected to ignore it all, bottle up his feelings. Why shouldn't they talk to each other, get to know one another? It wasn't fair. People should be free to be with just whoever they wanted. This world was so messed up by those who wanted to dictate how others should live.

His mother had told him there would be many times likes this. Times when he would have to ignore his feelings however strong they might be and submit to whatever white folk demanded. Fight the urge to show emotion, to resist. Just one step out of line was all it took. It could be something trivial but if a white man took offense at it, he could end up being killed, she had warned him.

At first, Thomas thought he must have been having a nightmare when they woke him in the middle of the night. He hit the floor with a thud as they unceremoniously tipped him out of his hammock before he could get out. It was hard to discern much in the shadows and the lantern one carried obscured his face, but once again his voice was enough to identify him. In his other hand Abraham carried a pistol. With his right foot he kicked Thomas hard in the ribs several times, making him curl up in pain.

"Get up, you filthy nigger."

Thomas struggled to his feet.

"What's happening? I ain't done nothing."

"You'd be lynched if you were on dry land. Attacking a young white woman like that."

"I never-"

"Shut up," said Abraham. "You can tell your lies to the judge. Won't make any difference though, you'll still hang for it."

Silenced, Thomas was dragged to the stern and chained to the rail. Abraham gave an order to the two men with him.

"You two stand guard until we dock in the morning. Don't let anyone speak to him."

Normally Thomas greeted the dawn as they

neared New Orleans with exaltation, looking forward to seeing his family and friends again. This time he resented the brashness of that morning's sunrise. The severity of the situation facing him had sunk in, leaving him drained and with a sense of utter hopelessness, unable to do anything to avoid the fate which awaited him.

Everybody knew that an accused black person was never found innocent. There would be the charade of justice, but there was no equality before the law whatever the Constitution might say. That battle had been lost when Reconstruction had ended and the South left in the hands of the former Confederates.

As soon as the boat berthed, two policemen arrived. Handcuffing him, they chained his feet together and marched him off, though all he could do was shuffle along awkwardly. Out of the corner of his eye, he saw Art and the other members of the band. There was sympathy in their expression but also a look of resignation. They had all been around long enough to know how just a few words from a white person could blow a life apart like a tornado hitting a house, smashing it into thousands of pieces.

Mosa, who'd left Maisie sleeping to come down to welcome her son, couldn't believe what her eyes were seeing. She made her way through the watching crowd to get near him.

"What's happening?"

"Stay back," commanded one of the policemen.

"I'm his mother."

"You can make inquiries at the Sheriff's office later this morning. Now stay back like I told you or I'll have you arrested."

The news they gave her that morning was worse than she'd feared. A young woman, Emily Adams, had been assaulted by someone in her cabin during the night. Thomas, they told her, was that person. Mosa's legs began trembling.

Outside she had to sit on the step, breathing in short bursts of anxiety. In her life she'd had plenty of sadness, lost many she'd loved, but life had continued and she had been blessed with her children. The prospect that she could be losing one to the hangman's noose was more than she could bear. Uncontrollable grunts of despair poured out of her before giving way to sobs. Passers-by crossed to the other side of the street. Maybe some wanted to give her space for her grief but too many shook their heads and rolled their eyes in undisguised disdain.

CHAPTER 30

As the shock faded a little, Mosa made her way back to Tremé. Angelique was on her way to school when she saw her and crossed the street.

"Whatever's the matter? You look like you've seen a ghost."

"It's Thomas. He's been arrested, accused of assaulting a white girl."

Angelique's mouth opened with horror.

"That can't be right. He'd never do a thing like that. Look, I've got to get to school now. I'll come round as soon as it finishes."

"Can you tell the kids there'll be no extra lessons this evening. I couldn't face it."

"Sure. I'll be back as soon as I can."

Maisie was waiting impatiently by the door when her mother got back to the house.

"Why ain't you at school? Go."

"I wanted to see Thomas."

"Thomas had work to do. He's had to stay on board. You'll get to see him next time. Now scat."

"Hmm." Maisie stomped off in a huff, but soon broke into a run when she saw friends come

DAVID CANFORD

around the corner ahead of her.

Mosa spent the day inside, seeking refuge in the shadows. If she went out, she'd have to say hello to all those to who this bright, sunny day was a reason to be happy. When late afternoon Angelique came, Mosa dissolved into tears in her arms.

"They're gonna hang him. Hang my only son."

"Don't think like that. We'll get him a good lawyer."

"You're right," said Mosa, temporary hope reflected in her eyes. "I can sell this place, sell everything we have. But even that won't be enough will it? No lawyer can save my son. Whatever he says, no white jury is gonna believe him. It's hopeless."

"You mustn't think like that. We'll figure something out. Just leave it to me. I'll be back later. Can I fix you something to eat before I go?"

"I'm not hungry, but thanks for offering."

It was gone nightfall when Angelique returned. Mosa was sitting alone in the dark. Angelique lit the lamp, revealing the man who accompanied her.

"Who's this?"

"Don't you recognize me, Miss Elwood?"

The man was dressed in a suit and wore an earnest expression.

"Samuel?"

"Yes, ma'am."

"He's just passed the Bar. He's going to help us," said Angelique.

189

"I'll pay you as soon as I can sell the house."

"There's no need. You've spent your life helping others, now it's your turn to be helped. Without your teaching I never would've gotten to be an attorney. I'll go down to the courthouse in the morning and then try to get to see Thomas."

"Can you save my boy?"

"I'll do everything that I possibly can."

He returned the following evening.

"I got to see Thomas. He sends his love."

"How is he?"

"He's doing OK. He's due in court tomorrow. The accusation is that he'd been bothering an Emily Adams who was traveling down from Memphis with her family, that he made his way up to the first class deck after dark, broke into her cabin and tried to rape her."

"It can't be true, I know my son. What does Thomas say?"

"That it's untrue. He says he did speak to her briefly when she came down onto the lower deck, but a white crew member told her she shouldn't be down there and escorted her away. That was the last he saw of her. I should go now to prepare for tomorrow. The hearing's at ten if you want to attend."

"Of course I do. I want to be there to support him."

"I wish I could come too," said Angelique. "But I'll be in school."

"That's fine. I'll be all right. And thanks, Angelique, for finding Samuel. I really appreciate it."

Not long after they left, Mosa received another visitor. It was Lowenna. Mosa burst into tears again.

"Oh Mosa, what's wrong?"said Lowenna putting her arms around her."I'll come with you tomorrow. You shouldn't have to do this alone," she said after Mosa had explained.

CHAPTER 31

The judge sat in front of the Louisiana seal, a pelican protecting her chicks on the nest with the words "Justice, Union and Confidence". To his side stood the Louisiana flag of similar design in white and blue, and the Stars and Stripes. The display gave the illusion of a place of fairness, where impartial justice would be dispensed.

Mosa gasped as Thomas was brought in, his chains clanking. His face was bruised and swollen from a beating, probably more than one. He took a seat beside Samuel. Asked to stand and plead, he pleaded not guilty.

"Does Counsel for the prosecution or defense have any preliminary issues they wish to raise?" asked the judge.

The prosecuting attorney shook his head, but Samuel got up.

"Your Honor, I note the only two witnesses for the prosecution will be the victim's father and an Abraham Gillingham."

Mosa and Lowenna exchanged looks of surprise at hearing that name.

"That is correct."

"I wish to ask that the victim herself be called as a witness, and for a subpoena to be issued if she refuses."

"Request denied. The poor young lady has suffered more than enough already."

"But your Honor-"

"No more. I have made my ruling. Let's proceed."

After the all white jury had been sworn in, Mr. Adams took the stand.

"Sir, could you describe what happened on the night in question," asked the prosecutor.

"My wife and I were in bed when our daughter burst into our cabin. She was in a state of utter distress. Her nightgown was torn. She told us a man had attacked her in her cabin. I immediately threw some clothes on over my pajamas and found the captain. He was as horrified as we were, and said he would investigate immediately. I returned to our cabin to comfort my daughter. When she had calmed down a little, I suggested she sleep with my wife, and I went to sleep in her cabin, though as you can imagine sleep for all of us that night was most difficult."

"Thank you, sir. I have no more questions."

Samuel stood.

"Sir, did your daughter offer any description of her attacker."

"No, it was dark. However, she was convinced by the smell of him that he was most certainly a Negro."

"It is unfortunate we are not able to confirm that with her."

The judge brought his gavel down, his face a cauldron of rage.

"Mr. Scott, I will not warn you again. How dare you imply that Mr. Adams, a respected member of our community, is not telling the truth. Next witness."

Abraham was wearing his uniform of dark navy blue and shining gold buttons, so upstanding and trustworthy looking compared to Thomas in his prison uniform of horizontal black and white stripes. At the prosecutor's request, Abraham recounted his version of events.

"I was walking the decks in the early evening when I encountered the defendant harassing the victim."

"How exactly?"

"He said he had another tune he must play for her on his trumpet. She told him no, but he grabbed her arm. I intervened. He had that look in his eye that male Negroes get, like a wild animal in the mating season."

"Objection, your Honor," said Samuel jumping to his feet.

"Overruled. Please continue, Mr. Gillingham."

"He called after her as I led her away. Said he'd come play for her later. When I'd escorted her back to the upper deck, I returned to tell him his behavior was unacceptable and that he was fired. He was furious and began shouting at me, telling me white folk had it coming to them, especially our women. I must confess that given his impudence and ugly threats, I couldn't help myself. I struck him across the face."

The prosecutor gave a nod of smug satisfaction in Samuel's direction as he came forward to question. Samuel probed Abraham, trying all the while to get him to contradict himself and give some basis to challenge his evidence as untruthful.

"Mr. Gillingham, why would the defendant, or any person of color for that matter, say such things? We all know the consequences likely to befall anyone who did."

"I don't know. I too was shocked. I've never heard a nigger speak like that. He seemed crazed. Like there was nothing that would stop him carrying out his threat."

"So thinking that, did you warn the victim or her father, or indeed the captain or any other member of the crew?"

"I patrolled the upper deck after dinner and then went down to check that the defendant was asleep. He appeared to be. Clearly that was all an act and he went up later."

"Why would he be crazed as you claim? He had an exemplary record and a good job. Why would he put all that in jeopardy by acting in the way which you have described?"

"I can't say, maybe you should ask him."

"Were you perhaps irritated, enraged even, by seeing the victim talking to him and appearing to enjoy his playing?"

"Absolutely not. I could tell she was frightened, that's why I moved in."

"Where were they standing when you arrived on deck?"

"He was standing in front of her, blocking her way."

"So how could you see that she was frightened?"

"I..."

"You are harassing the witness. We have heard enough," intervened the judge. "We will reconvene tomorrow when Counsel may give their closing arguments."

Mosa and Lowenna were standing outside the courtroom when Abraham emerged. Her cheeks turning pink with anger, Lowenna went over to confront him.

"You were lying in there, Abe. I know you were. You forget, I'm your mother. I've always been able to tell whether you were telling the truth. Why are you doing this?"

"Get out of my way. I know what you are. You disgust me."

Abraham pushed past her and strode out.

CHAPTER 32

"I should go talk with Samuel. I'll see you tomorrow," said Mosa.

Lowenna appeared distracted, her hand across her mouth, an elbow resting on her other arm which was placed horizontally across her waist.

"Oh...yes."

Seeing Adams leaving the building, she followed him along the street and all the way to the Garden District. He turned and went up the front steps into a distinctive gothic mansion painted in pale blue with three gable end roofs.

Lowenna halted. She breathed in deeply, trying to summon the courage needed and hoping that he wouldn't be the one to open the door. Now she remembered why he seemed familiar to her. The man had been a customer on more than one occasion.

It was the maid who opened the door.

"Hello, I was wondering if I might have a word with Miss Adams."

"Who is it?" called her father's voice. Adams appeared in the hallway. "You may go," he said to the maid. Once she had gone through a door at the end of the corridor, he turned on Lowenna. "How dare you come here. Get off my property at once or I'll have you arrested."

"Sir, Abraham Gillingham, as he now calls himself, is my son. I know he's lying. A terrible injustice is about to happen. Only your daughter can stop it occurring."

The door slammed shut in her face. Dispirited, Lowenna departed. She turned only once as she walked down the pathway when she heard a door closing and looked up to the second floor balcony. No one was there.

A palpable air of excitement emanating from the white audience filled the courtroom the following morning. Justice was about to be done and soon there'd be a hanging to go see.

Mosa sat at the back, desolate and alone. Lowenna hadn't come, though that wasn't the thought which was exercising her mind. She was praying for a miracle to save Thomas.

As the judge entered, Mosa's heartbeat tripled. If only she could take the punishment for her son. He was so young with all his life in front of him. What a terrible twist of fate that Lloyd and Lowenna's son should be the one whose testimony would convict Thomas.

It would be a lynching in all but name. There would be no justice. The judge was unashamedly biased as was the entire legal system.

Mosa didn't know how she was going to go forward from here. Her whole life it seemed had been one of constant battles, one after another, a never ending struggle. At times, the promise of a better tomorrow had been dangled in front of her. Each time it had been snatched away. She'd had to be strong for too long. Mosa was worn out, her zest for life had run dry. She didn't think she had the strength to climb over the mountain of grief looming on her horizon.

The closing submissions were about to begin when the large double wooden doors at the rear opened. All eyes turned, curious to see who was this latecomer who dared to interrupt proceedings. A young woman entered and began making her way to the front. Her eyes darted around, betraying her nervousness in this unfamiliar and intimidating environment.

"Take a seat Miss," commanded the judge. "This court is already in session."

Her voice was faint. Mosa leaned forward, straining to hear her words.

"Please, sir, I am Emily Adams. I wish to give evidence."

People exchanged looks of silent pleasure. Things were about to get even more interesting than they thought. They loved a drama.

"There is no need. No need to put yourself through that. We have heard all we need to. Now do sit down before I have you removed."

She had reached the front. This time her voice was clearer and stronger.

"But it wasn't that man," she said pointing at Thomas. "When the man left after attacking me, I saw the color of his skin in the moonlight as he opened the door. He was white."

An audible intake of breath swept through the courtroom like a strong gust of wind. Those attending couldn't restrain themselves and an enormous hubbub erupted. Mosa flung her head back and closed her eyes in relief.

"Order! Order!"

When silence returned, the judge requested Emily Adams to take the stand. The prosecutor had no questions for her. All that needed to be said already had been. The judge had no option.

"I find that there is no case to answer. The defendant is to be released. Jurors, I thank you for your service."

Mosa made her way to the front against the crush of those leaving. She hugged her son and Samuel.

"Thank you, Samuel. Thank you so much."

"There's really nothing to thank me for. That was a mighty close run thing. If Emily hadn't showed up, there would've been a guilty verdict for sure. I don't know how she came to be here. It must have been providence. I'll escort Thomas back to the jail to get his clothes and then send him home."

"I'm going to cook a special dinner tonight. I hope you will join us."

"Thanks. I'll definitely be there."

The news of the acquittal spread like wildfire. When Mosa got back to Tremé, there was already a throng of people waiting. Angelique was amongst them and ran up to embrace her.

"We're all so happy for you. I sent the kids home. Today's a day for celebrating. We're gonna party tonight, put on a real Tremé welcome for Thomas."

That evening the streets echoed with the sound of music and hand clapping as everyone who wasn't too young or too old to stand danced their hearts out. The biggest cheers were reserved for Thomas ad-libbing on his trumpet.

When a moment finally came that Mosa wasn't a focus of attention, she slipped away heading south.

She found her, sitting on a bench. The hunched shoulders and head hung down spoke of a torment within. Mosa sat down quietly next to her and touched her hand.

"Mosa?" Words then gushed out of Lowenna like a levee broken by the force of floodwater. "I'm so sorry. So sorry that my son would do this. I was too ashamed to come to court today. It's all my fault. It's OK for you to hate me. I've brought you nothing but trouble. It was me that made Abe like this by lying to him about where he came from. I've let everybody down.

"I tried to help, but I mess up everything I do. I followed Adams home. Asked to speak to his daughter, to beg her to come give evidence to stop a terrible injustice, but he threw me out."

Her voice faltered.

"It was you."

"Me?"

"You saved my son, Lowenna. His daughter must have heard what you said. She turned up at the courthouse this morning. Said it was a white man who attacked her. Thomas is free."

"Really?"

"Yes, really. Now come with me. We're having the party of the year and I want you to be there."

The two women walked off arm in arm. As they entered Congo Square, they heard the music coming from Tremé. Almost imperceptibly at first, they began swaying. By the time they had crossed the Square, they no longer held each other by the arm. Moving in unison, they were laughing and clapping to the beat.

+ + + + + + + + + + + + + + + +

ALSO BY DAVID CANFORD

The Throwback

The prequel to Sweet Bitter Freedom.

Bound Bayou

A young teacher from England achieves a dream when he gets the chance to work for a year in the United States, but 1950s Mississippi is not the America he has seen on the movie screens at home. When his independent spirit collides with the rules of life in the Deep South, he sets off a chain of events he can't control.

Kurt's War

Kurt is an English evacuee with a difference. His father is a Nazi. As Kurt grows into an adult and is forced to pretend that he is someone he isn't for his own protection, can he survive in the hostile world in which he must live? And with his enemies closing in, will even the woman he loves believe who he really is?

A Heart Left Behind

New Yorker, Orla, finds herself trapped in a web of secret love, blackmail and espionage in the build up to WWII. Moving to Berlin and hoping to escape her past, she is forced to undertake a life-threatening task to try and save not just herself but also her son.

Betrayal in Venice

Sent to Venice on a secret mission against the Nazis, a soldier finds his life unexpectedly altered when he saves a young woman at the end of the Second World War. Many years later, Glen Butler discovers the truth. His reaction betrays the one he loves most, his daughter.

Going Big or Small

A Man Called Ove meets Thelma and Louise as British humour collides with European culture. Retiree, Frank, gets more adventure than he bargained for when he sets off across 1980s Europe hoping to shake up his mundane life. Falling in love with a woman and Italy has unexpected consequences.

A Good Nazi? The Lies We Keep

Growing up in 1930s Germany two boys, one Catholic and one Jewish, become close friends. After Hitler seizes power, their lives are changed forever. When World War 2 comes, will they help each other, or will secrets from their teenage years make them enemies?

When the Water Runs out

Will water shortage result in the USA invading Canada? One person can stop a war if he isn't killed first, but is he a hero or a traitor? When two very different worlds collide, the outcome is on a knife-edge.

2045 The Last Resort

In 2045 those who lost their jobs to robots are taken care of in resorts where life is an endless vacation. For those still in work, the American dream has never been better. But is all quite as perfect as it seems?

Sea Snakes and Cannibals

A travelogue of visits to islands across the globe, including remote Fijian islands, Corsica, the Greek islands and islands in the Sea of Cortez, Mexico.

SIGN UP

Don't forget to sign up to receive David Canford's email newsletter at David.Canford.com including information on new releases and promotions and claim your free ebook

ABOUT THE AUTHOR

David started writing stories for his grandmother as a young boy. They usually involved someone being eaten by a monster of the deep, with his grandmother often the hapless victim.

Years later as chair lady of her local Women's Institute, David's account of spending three days on a Greyhound bus crossing the United States from the west coast to the east coast apparently saved the day when the speaker she had booked didn't show up.

David's life got busy after university and he stopped writing until the bug got him again recently.

As an indie author himself, David likes discovering the wealth of great talent which is now so easily accessible. A keen traveller, he can find a book on travel particularly hard to resist.

He enjoys writing about both the past and what might happen to us in the future.

Cambridge University educated, his previous jobs include working as a mover in Canada and a sandblaster in the Rolls Royce aircraft engine factory. David works as a lawyer during the day. He has three daughters and lives on the south coast of England with his wife and their dog.

A lover of both the great outdoors and the man-made world, he is equally happy kayaking, hiking a trail or wandering around a city absorbing its culture.

You can contact him by visiting his website at DavidCanford.com